THE CIRCUS OF
STOLEN DREAMS

THE CIRCUS OF STOLEN DREAMS

LORELEI SAVARYN

PHILOMEL BOOKS

PHILOMEL BOOKS

An imprint of Penguin Random House LLC, New York

First published in the United States of America by Philomel,
an imprint of Penguin Random House LLC, 2020.

Philomel Books is a registered trademark of Penguin Random House LLC.

Visit us online at penguinrandomhouse.com

Library of Congress Cataloging-in-Publication Data is available.

Printed in the United States of America

ISBN 9780593202067

1 3 5 7 9 10 8 6 4 2

Edited by Liza Kaplan.
Design by Monique Sterling.
Text set in Charter.

Chapter opener art: Branches illustration by leeyenz, 123Rf.com.

To Felicity, August, Mary, and Zelie:
May you always be dreamers.

THE GIRL WITHOUT A SHADOW

The dining room window reflected the blurred façade of a happy family at dinner: a mom and dad and their one and only child. Andrea glared through the silent, transparent scene, up at the moon and the way it shone like a spotlight, piercing them with its otherworldly glow.

Family dinners used to be loud. Francis would tell jokes from his joke book and make ridiculous noises just to get Andrea to laugh. Andrea would cut in, the words pouring out of her like water in a swift current as she told them all every single detail about her day. Their mom and dad would look at each other, their faces a mixture of wide eyes and amused smiles.

Now no one, not her parents sitting next to her at the table, not the blurred family in the window, not even the man in the moon knew what to do other than steep in the silence.

Andrea stabbed a piece of chicken.

Her mother put her fork down and folded her hands as if in prayer, giving a slight nudge of the elbow to her father. "Just tell her," she whispered, as if Andrea couldn't hear.

Her father shuffled carrots around his plate, then cleared his throat. "Your mother and I . . . We know this hasn't been easy on you."

Andrea's breathing grew shallow. She curled her fingers into a ball, pressing her nails hard into her palms, making mini moon marks against her skin.

"But we think it's time to let go," he continued. "Winter's coming. Your mother could use the space in the garage."

"And we think it would be healthy, Drea." Her mother stared empty-eyed at the wood grain on the table. "We'd like you to go through his boxes and choose a few things you'd like to keep."

Any food Andrea had already eaten formed itself into a knot in her stomach, threatening to make its way back up.

Her father reached out a hand to touch her shoulder, but Andrea recoiled, pressing her back into her chair. For the past three years, Andrea had blamed him for everything: for the divorce, for showing up on Sunday nights and making them sit through Fake Family Dinner. She had even tried to blame him for what happened to Francis. But, as always, the steady

2

pulsing rhythm of blame grew a little louder from a dark place deep inside.

Your fault, your fault, your fault.

Andrea tilted her chair away from the empty seat at the end of the table. "I'm not ready." She tried the three words that had gotten her out of so much since it happened. Homework, soccer, talking about the night Francis disappeared. She didn't want to go through her brother's things, but the thought of the boxes being discarded unseen scrubbed at Andrea's scabbed-over wounds like an eraser, hot with friction.

"*I* can't keep looking at them every time I walk in the garage," her mother snapped, her voice cracking on the last word, ripping *garage* right in half like it was a piece of paper. "Someone is coming to pick them up tomorrow. You don't have to go through them. We just wanted to let you know. It's time."

Her father drummed his fingers on the tabletop, then sighed. "Thanks for dinner, Sus," he said, picking up his plate and carrying it to the kitchen.

Her mother watched Andrea with dark, sad eyes, and her mouth fell open for a moment like she was about to say something else. Instead, she picked up her own plate and followed him, her shoulders curved inward as if the air had been sucked straight out of her chest.

"Fine, I'll look," Andrea said, tossing her crumpled napkin on her plate, though there was no one left to hear her. There was just the silent house, weighted with the words no one had been able to say, for so much longer than the three years Francis had been gone.

***

Andrea ran up to her room as soon as her father's engine faded down the street, which had followed the stiff hugs and the *see you laters* and the *love you, kiddos*—her father's faltering attempts to bridge the gap that had formed between them. She sat on the floor, her back to the bottom bunk, hugging a gray pillow shaped like a star against her chest and staring at the bookshelf against the opposite wall. Gathering her strength. Her parents made it sound so easy. Like sending Francis's belongings away on a donation truck would somehow fix things. Like erasing the evidence her brother had existed would take away the pain of how he disappeared.

Andrea wished every single day that she could erase the terrible thing that had happened and the relentless, silent guilt she carried on her shoulders, but never once had she wanted to erase Francis. He had been her little shadow. Andrea smiled now at all the times he had annoyed her, like when he followed her on a bike ride, his tiny little legs pedaling so hard to keep up as she fell to a painfully slow pace so she wouldn't leave him behind. She had read *Peter Pan* once and couldn't understand why the boy was so desperate to have Wendy sew his annoying shadow back onto his feet.

She understood now.

No matter what other people did, Andrea would never forget her brother, even though so many others had chosen that as their way to navigate the strangeness of a boy who had disappeared from his room in the middle of the night. The kids who changed the subject when Andrea mentioned Francis's name, the neighbor who once stupidly said how lucky Andrea was to not have to share. And now, this—her parents giving away all his things. She would hold him inside the hollow space in her heart created by the Great Missing. Her heart would shout: *He was here. He was here.*

Andrea's mom shuffled by in the hall a few moments later, poking her head inside the door. "I'm going to watch TV for a bit in my room," she said, resting her fingers along the doorframe. "Let me know if you need anything, okay?"

"Okay."

"I love you."

Her mom's *I love yous* came too fast and too often. They tilted up at the end like a question, an unspoken pleading for reassurance that somehow, even after all that had happened, she hadn't let Andrea down.

Andrea hugged the pillow a little tighter. Of course she loved her mom, but sometimes, saying so was hard for her now.

"I love you, too," Andrea said, just loud enough to be heard.

Her mom exhaled, the kind of exhale that was saturated in relief. She walked away, clicking Andrea's bedroom door shut behind her.

Andrea stayed until she heard the familiar muffled sound of her mother surfing through TV channels before dropping the pillow and padding down the stairs and to the garage. She might as well get this over with, so at least she could say that she tried.

She flipped on the switch, giving her eyes a moment to adjust to the unforgiving yellow light. An electric hum buzzed from the bulb above her head and she walked, slow and tentative, like the floor might break away underneath her, toward the pile in the corner she had ignored for three whole years.

Seven stacked, unlabeled cardboard boxes contained nearly all of Francis's belongings. Unlike some parents when their kid goes missing, Andrea's mother had packed everything up in a flurry the day after snow dusted the earth and the trails had all run cold and the police told them they were

6

calling off the local search. They concluded that someone had climbed up their trellis, slipped in through their open bedroom window, and taken Francis away in the night.

In response to the news, her mom had blazed through their house, unable to stand the thought of sitting still and desperate to keep her hands moving as she tried to add a hint of order to the chaos. Since then, Andrea had caught her mom glimpsing at the boxes with regret each time they got into the car, but no one ever touched them.

Andrea ran her hand along one of the tops, leaving a path through the dust. The logical side of her knew none of this was the boxes' fault, but she hated them just the same. Hated what they stood for. That there was a reason they were here, full of her brother's stuff while his half of their room sat empty.

Empty because of her.

A tentative finger slid under one of the box's folded flaps, popping it open. Inside rested dozens of objects: Francis's favorite framed pictures, a stray blue sock, a miniature slinky.

Andrea reached down and pressed her pale hand firmly against the pocket of her jeans, reassured at the outline of the small item resting carefully inside it. Her parents didn't know that she had already kept something precious of her brother's. That she kept it with her at all times.

It was such a ridiculous little thing to keep, but Andrea

didn't care that it didn't make sense. Her parents had done all sorts of things that didn't make sense in the months after Francis disappeared. Her mother had slept with his blanket tucked tight around her. Her father had sat in the living room watching football, unblinking, like a zombie, like he still lived in their house.

It was her very last connection to her brother. The day he disappeared, Andrea had tucked the trinket away in her pocket, hoping against hope that Francis had left her some sort of secret clue, something that would help her find him.

It had turned out to be useless. But it was still the last thing he had left behind.

In the box, the ghosts of who they all used to be stared up at Andrea with frozen smiles on their faces in brightly colored frames, a brazen reminder of how much they had lost. In one picture, taken at a photo studio inside a department store on a mild spring day, the family posed in coordinating outfits of blue jeans and white T-shirts, a similar outfit to the one Andrea wore now. They had gone out for milkshakes after to celebrate, and both Andrea and Francis ordered a large, *promising* their parents they'd finish the whole thing. But little stomachs fill quickly, and instead of letting the shakes go to waste, their dad insisted on finishing them off. They watched in awe as he braced himself, refusing to stand until he had swallowed the last drop. He was the dad with three full milk-shakes rolling around in his belly and he definitely played up the part, making them all laugh with loud gurgling noises and exaggerated warnings that if they didn't hold his trembling stomach together, he might explode in front of their very eyes.

The air in the garage pressed heavy against Andrea's chest, growing tighter by the second.

"I'm sorry," she said to the boxes, pushing down the lump in her throat. "I can't look anymore." Her one item would have to be enough. She couldn't bear the weight of carrying any more pieces of her missing brother inside her pockets.

Andrea backed away and grabbed hold of her bike where it stood propped against the garage wall. She strapped on her helmet and pushed down, sinking the heels of her shoes heavily on the pedals. She rode past the house of nosy Ms. Penelope, the lady who brought them tins of cookies and too often peeked outside at the world through her large window. She passed a game of kickball being played on a side street by a bunch of neighbor kids, most of whom had little siblings sitting on the curb chewing on ropes of taffy candy. Someone shouted out to her, but Andrea pretended she didn't hear. She rode past row after row of houses settling into the silence of night, pedaling farther and farther down the street and away from her house until her thighs and calves burned. Then she pushed some more.

Going through Francis's boxes wouldn't fix any of the things that had broken. But she could feel the crisp fall breeze on her face, and she could fly like the wind on her bike. She could imagine she was somewhere far, far away. Somewhere bad things didn't happen. Somewhere brothers didn't disappear.

It was a game she played with herself. If she rode fast enough, maybe she could outrun the sadness, the guilt, the pain of a cracked heart. If she rode fast enough, maybe she wouldn't break.

FORGET YOUR TROUBLES

Andrea biked past where the road ended and onto a trail that ran over a small bridge and through a park before finally giving way to a dark, thick wood. Memories lurked everywhere in this place, especially now with the trees tinted orange. She and Francis had spent many afternoons playing in the park when they were smaller, going down slides, sharing Goldfish crackers, and getting their parents to give them underdogs on the swings.

There were also the nightmares Francis used to have about this place. Nightmares about a river and an evil tree determined to turn him into stone. Francis dealt with more nightmares than she ever had, and this had been a recurring one. It clung to Andrea, made the hair on the back of her neck stand on end as if the nightmare had been hers, too.

Once she crossed into the forest, the moonlight shone brightly enough to light Andrea's way, but even if it hadn't, she knew the path by heart. Eventually it would curve around and spit her out back near her home, but not before it wound through groves of trees and shallow ravines and a quiet, empty field where deer would rest in the sun during the day.

The air around Andrea buzzed, almost electric, like lightning might strike at any moment, though above her hovered a cloudless sky. The leaves left on the trees took on a silvery shine, washed in the moon's light. The woods wore the scent of velvety secrets and sadness blanketed by something sweet, like a box of her mother's dark chocolate.

Andrea drew in one long, deep breath, letting the calm of the forest at nightfall weave its way through her. Her heart, mind, and pace slowed, until she became as still and quiet as the stars that hung above her head.

She hopped off her bike and propped the kickstand, then cast her gaze around the woods, landing on a soft column of glow. The moon had shifted its unforgiving spotlight off her and onto a gnarled old tree near the path, rough and widened with age. Its knobby limbs twisted upward like fingers, bending to the sky. On its wrist-like trunk hung a single piece of parchment, fluttering as if desperate to break free.

Fresh-fallen leaves crunched under Andrea's sneakers as she moved toward the tree. Her mind flashed back to the flyers for her brother they had plastered up all around town within hours of finding him gone, stapling his picture to poles and taping it to shopwindows. His face flashed nightly on the news, and in online searches beneath the word *Missing* and a phone number for the police. Andrea half expected this to be another one. A poster of Francis that had somehow survived three years of winters and spring rains, that had lasted long past when the neighbors stopped dropping casseroles off at the door and the news vans found other stories to tell. She paused, her shoes sinking into the soft, damp earth.

If it was Francis's face, faded and mottled with age, she didn't want to see it.

A sudden, cool breeze kicked up around her, sending branches bowing sideways. The poster tore free from the tree and flew, looping over and over in the air before sticking itself to Andrea's face, unwilling to be ignored. Andrea clawed at the paper, pulling it from her nose and cheeks. The wind died down to nothing and the woods hushed as Andrea took a reluctant peek at what she now held in her hands.

Thick and yellowed and curled in at the edges, the paper had the appearance of age, as if it had hung there for a hundred years or more. It shimmered gold, then silver, depending on which way the moonlight hit. Elaborate scrolling words framed the top and bottom of an image of sweeping striped circus tents surrounded by a sky full of twinkling stars.

Andrea covered her mouth with her hand as she lingered on a single phrase. *Forget your troubles.* She had tried so many things to help her deal with what had happened, like riding fast on her bike, or throwing herself into schoolwork, or sitting on a couch playing card games with Dr. Tammy, who asked too many questions and acted like they were friends.

The boxes in the garage had helped her deal with it, too. As long as the boxes sat there, Andrea was free to secretly dream that one day her brother might return home, somehow. She imagined her parents kept the boxes because they harbored a quiet faith, too. But now that her parents were giving away all of Francis's things, the final, unspoken hope the boxes represented floated away into the night sky, leaving her as empty as the corner in the garage would be once they were gone.

This was what she needed right now—to escape the pain. If it was possible, if the poster was real and she could actually forget her troubles, even for a little while, Andrea would accept the offer in a heartbeat.

Another breeze blew by, lifting leaves off the ground and swirling them around Andrea and the poster and the tree, ripping the poster from her fingers and sending it into the night sky.

The scent of pine needles and decaying leaves and the soil after a storm wasn't a surprise—Andrea was used to the smells of the forest from exploring and biking through them for so many years. But this tickling wind brought with it an aroma that belonged at the county fair instead of tucked away in the woods. Cotton candy and cinnamon. Nearly burnt caramel and crisp, red apples. Fresh-popped corn.

Whatever this was, something was happening. Something big. A pinprick of hope leapt up in Andrea's stomach as the moon lent a hypnotic yellow-green illumination to the wooded path ahead. She grabbed the handlebars of her bike and walked forward, following the moonlight up a hill and to the edge of the abandoned field.

But it wasn't abandoned anymore.

Andrea gasped, eyes wide, and dropped her bike to the dirt.

A wrought iron fence encircled the field. At the top of the fence, the tips of the posts splayed in every direction and a pointed star adorned the end of each, like hundreds of starbursts stretching to the sky. The fence culminated in a tall iron gate next to where Andrea stood. The iron twisted into a pattern of stars and one crescent moon, smiling like he kept a secret. Worked into the iron, over the gate in scrolling, glittering metal, was the word *Reverie*. And under it, in slightly smaller print: *Land of Dreams*.

The very air surrounding Reverie pulled her in, drew her to it like a magnet. She couldn't help but wonder if the circus had somehow sought her out and placed itself right where she would find it, though of course it was a silly thought. Circuses traveled from town to town, but not solely for the benefit of one single girl.

Andrea walked forward with cautious, measured steps until she reached the gate, a spark of energy taking hold inside her chest. Clutching clammy hands around the spindling metal, she peered through to what was inside, barely daring to blink as she took it all in.

Behind the gate, the world of Reverie buzzed with movement, with light. With people laughing, smiling, and eating cotton candy saturated with wild colors off striped sticks. Andrea pressed her forehead against the cold fence and squinted her eyes.

There was something . . . different about the crowd roaming inside the fence—people as young as three with bouncing, curly hair and others who were long and gangly-limbed and well into their teens. The group of revelers was built out of not just people but children. *Only* children. Not a single adult in sight.

Children ran and skipped through a long fairway lined with bright shops that led away from the gate. The windows of each shop bore large signs that promised an assortment of delectable treats. A pink-and-yellow storefront offered magical lollipops that had the power to make you dizzy in the best of ways. Another, right next to it, painted black as night, offered poisoned apples meant to turn the stomach of an enemy. Another, built of scrap wood, sold oddities—ground unicorn horn, bottled color extracted from rainbows, fossilized fairy wings. Andrea's grip tightened on the fence as her mind hummed, imagining what other wonders the rest of the shops would claim to hold.

Surrounding the fairway and spreading out in all

directions stood a seemingly endless array of tents. More tent tops spread to the horizon than should fit in the fenced-in space or within the bounds of the field. All striped the same color, alternating glittering-star bright and midnight blue, each tent drew gracefully upward to a single peak. At the topmost point of each waved a pennant flag, striped just the same.

Andrea pinched her arm, pulling the skin tight between her thumb and finger. If she was dreaming, she wouldn't feel an ounce of sting. She had done it dozens of times over the past three years—even pinching herself over and over again in the weeks after Francis disappeared. She had hoped she'd one day discover she'd only been trapped in a terrible, horrible dream and that when she woke up, she'd find Francis, sleeping and safe on the bottom bunk. But each and every time it hurt, and she had to realize anew that the nightmare of losing him had been—was still—real.

Now, standing outside Reverie's gates, the stinging of her skin more than answered her question. This place seemed almost impossible. Yet here it was, drawing her to it with the promise of forgetting, as real as anything she'd ever seen.

STEP RIGHT UP

"**C**ome to forget your troubles?"

Andrea startled as a smooth voice behind her broke the silence. She turned away from Reverie's gate to find a girl with a friendly-looking expression, about nine or ten years old, with a head full of long dark curls and a hand on her hip. She wore a bright red coat with tails and tight, black pants and shining riding boots, like she was the ringmaster of her own little circus. The girl tilted her chin upward, with a face so pale it almost shone silver in the light of the moon.

Andrea glanced back at the circus, whispering, almost pleading her answer. "Yes."

The girl giggled. "Of course you have. No one comes to Reverie by chance."

"But how is it possible?" Andrea asked. "How did it get here?"

"Reverie has always been there for those who need it, of

course. It's waiting for any child in desperate enough need of escape to find it. It's just around the bend of a curving mountain road, behind a shopping mall in a bustling city, and in the desert at the edge of a dusty old town. And right now, in these woods, it is here for you."

For her. And all those children running around inside Reverie's gates, each with some trouble they longed to forget. Andrea had so often assumed that others didn't have it as bad. So many of the kids she knew had lives that seemed nearly perfect, had hearts that seemed whole. Knowing that she and the children inside Reverie had something so huge in common made Andrea feel less alone, and braver, somehow.

The girl reached forward, offering Andrea her hand. "Come along now. I'm going to show you how to get your ticket. I'm Margaret Grace."

"I'm Andrea," she said, her fingers twitching at her sides. "But I don't have any money for a ticket."

Margaret Grace stifled another laugh with a pale palm. "Oh, we use something ever so much better than money. Come away with us, Andrea," she said softly. Her lips pulled upward in a gentle smile, revealing a set of deep dimples, one for each cheek. Her almost black eyes opened wide in expectation, like chocolate cookies in a sea of white milk. "It's all right. Take my hand. It's time to play."

Andrea wanted *in*. This could be exactly what she needed. To forget. To let the guilt, and the empty seat at the dining room table, and the sadness of losing her brother fall away and disappear. She didn't even glance back at the woods from where she came. She took hold of Margaret Grace's hand and let her lead the way.

***

Each of Margaret Grace's thin fingers burned Andrea's skin with cold, as if she were holding on to an icicle. She clenched her teeth, hoping to learn how to get her ticket before her fingers turned blue from frostbite.

Hidden in the shadows of the forest just out of sight from the gates stood a wooden booth, as golden and shining as the star on the top of a Christmas tree. A sign in scrolling print that matched the poster on the tree read *Tickets*. Margaret Grace gave Andrea a reassuring glance and led her a bit farther into the darkened woods. Andrea followed until they reached a grove shrouded in moonglow where a hammock that could have been made out of Rumpelstiltskin's thread rested, strung between two silver, lanky birch trees almost emptied of leaves.

"The cost of admission is one dream," Margaret Grace whispered, like she was imparting an exciting and valuable secret. "But it's not such a price to pay, as you can experience it anytime you like in a dream tent. It's how we keep Reverie growing and changing. Some children who come here choose to give up a good dream, so they can live it again and again inside Reverie's walls. Some children, though, give up a nightmare, so it can be gone and forgotten."

Margaret Grace leaned in closer, her voice almost too quiet to be heard.

"And some give up a *memory*. It works the same as dreams, and it can be a good memory or a bad one. You can relive it in Reverie or you can let it be gone. *Forgotten*, for the entire time you're here." With that last word she let go of Andrea's hand.

Andrea stilled, her breath hitching in her chest. She didn't want to exhale, shatter the fragile potential contained inside this moment, break whatever spell this girl had spun.

Margaret Grace exhaled and smiled. "Now then. We put you to sleep here for a moment." She pointed to the hammock hanging between the trees. You give us one dream, then wake up with a ticket to *all* the dreams you could ever hope to have."

Andrea stuffed her frozen fingers into her pocket, wrapping them around the small item that she had kept hidden inside. Everything about her life had grown so awful. The boxes in the garage. The empty seat at the table. The unrelenting guilt.

She would never forget Francis, but she could forget the reason for all her guilt and sadness. She could forget the night he disappeared.

A wide smile spread over Margaret Grace's face. "You're ready, aren't you?"

Andrea nodded, the memory she needed to give up clawing deep inside her. She would do anything to forget that night, even for a little while.

Before Margaret Grace could direct her, Andrea climbed into the hammock and rested her body inside it. Margaret Grace knelt to the earth next to Andrea's head and lifted up the bottom of her shirt to reveal a small leather pouch. "Now you must name your dream. We put the names of the dreams outside the tents so children get a hint at what they'll find inside."

Andrea lowered her head and stared through a gap in the trees at the twinkling white dots of light far above her in the blackened sky. The lump formed in her throat again and she fought once more to swallow it down. Surely she could face her memory long enough to name it. The pulsing voice inside her hummed a hungry, longing rhythm, nearly free of any hint of blame for the first time in three years.

It murmured softly. *Relief. Relief. Relief.*

Andrea's voice wavered. *"The Night You Left Us."*

Margaret Grace followed Andrea's eyes to the night sky and nodded slowly. "Very, very good."

Opening the pouch, Margaret Grace pulled out a pinch of a substance and released it into her palm, revealing hundreds of grains of glittering silver sand.

"Now close your eyes and repeat after me," Margaret Grace said. "I ask the Sandman."

"I ask the Sandman."

"To take me away."

"To take me away."

"To a land of dreams, in which I can play."

"To a land of dreams, in which I can play."

Margaret Grace sprinkled the sand over Andrea's closed eyes, and Andrea's mind grew slippery, thoughts shifting against one another and then falling away. There was something about the sand itself. Something about the way it glimmered. Something she wanted to hold on to.

But it was too late. Because at that exact moment, Andrea fell into a deep and deathlike sleep.

THE RULES

Andrea shot upright, half expecting to wake in her room. That Margaret Grace, the lights of Reverie, the strange leather pouch would have all been a bizarre dream, even though she had pinched herself outside the circus gates. But the hammock surged to one side, forcing Andrea to grasp at its golden braided edges. She gripped them tightly until the swaying slowed to a stop. Once stilled, Andrea reached up toward her eyes, which watered and stung like something sat stuck inside them. An eyelash, a piece of dust . . .

Grains of silver sand.

Andrea rubbed at her eyes, fast and hard, until the few remaining grains fell out and dropped to the forest floor. It had definitely, actually happened. She was really here.

In those brief, fleeting moments between the sleeping world and the world of the awake, Andrea could still feel the fragments of the memory she had lost as the price of her admission. It was less a feeling of an existing thing than an awareness that something was gone. A hole lived inside her now that she couldn't quite account for, as if she'd lost a piece of a puzzle to a dark and dusty corner. According to Margaret Grace, whatever she had lost would be used for Reverie, become a dream tent that children could experience if they so chose.

Andrea swung her legs over the side of the hammock and found the ground with her feet, lighter than before, like gravity bound her a bit less tightly to the earth. She shook her head, flinging off the grogginess that stuck to her mind like a crawling fog until her gaze landed on a leather pocket nailed to one of the birch trees nearby.

A piece of parchment rested inside it, which glowed, slightly, in the light of the full moon. Andrea snatched it from the pouch.

Printed in deep blue ink, the ticket read:

ADMISSION TO REVERIE
"LAND OF DREAMS"
ONE NIGHT ONLY
PAID IN FULL

Her ticket to Reverie.

She had done it. She had earned her ticket inside.

Andrea lifted her face toward the noise up ahead and marched to the ticket booth.

"Welcome to Reverie," Margaret Grace said, her eyes gleaming. She held out her palm. "Ticket, please."

Andrea handed over her ticket. Margaret Grace looked it over with approving, hungry eyes, then tucked it somewhere under the counter and folded her hands over the edge of the opening in the booth.

"There are a few rules that you must agree to before entering Reverie," she said. "Nothing too alarming, but make sure you pay attention and follow them for the ultimate Reverie experience. One," she held up a single finger. "Reverie is a land of dreams. It is *very* important that you remember that. Sometimes dreams can feel very real. Two," she held up a second finger. "The dreams are what they are; they're already in place. Don't go thinking you can change what happens in them, because you can't. Think of them like a ride at a theme park. In some dreams you have choices, but you're always following a track. You follow the track, you'll find the exit. Three," a third finger joined the other two. "Whatever you do, don't stay too long in a nightmare. And, lastly," she added a fourth and final finger. "Don't try to remember the dream you gave up for admission without going through its tent."

"Why not?" Andrea asked, confused. "And what do you mean about the nightmares?"

Margaret Grace offered Andrea a reassuring smile. "It's the rules, darling, and dreams can be tricky. Nightmares can be fun, but if you stay too long inside one, or try to remember the price of admission you just paid without going through the tent it turned into, it can cause your mind to react in some strange, strange ways. Things get rather . . . confusing, and nothing good can ever come of that. Of course, nightmares can also be fun, but if you're in one, make sure you get out quickly. And if you want to remember what you gave up to enter, simply find the tent and go in."

"I won't break the rules," Andrea said, trying to keep her voice steady. She was sure she wouldn't want to end up in any nightmares if she could help it, and she was even more certain she would have no reason to remember whatever she had been so eager to forget.

"Wonderful." Margaret Grace beamed. "Then just sign the waiver." She held out a clipboard with a gaudy feather pen attached by a string. "This says that you've heard the rules and understand it's your responsibility to follow them. And that it isn't our fault if you make a mistake."

Andrea signed her name without hesitation.

Margaret Grace looked over Andrea's signature

approvingly. "Now then, I think it's time, don't you?"

Andrea nodded, her eyes wide and her heart yearning to immerse itself in the promises of a night of escape.

Margaret Grace hopped out of the booth, and both girls walked with purposeful strides toward Reverie's gate, stopping next to a wide metal lever stuck into the earth.

"Welcome to Reverie," Margaret Grace said as she pulled back the lever. Andrea watched as Reverie's impressive gates opened with a giant creak.

The warmth and buzz and delicious aromas of Reverie wound around Andrea and seeped through her lungs and the pores of her skin, filling her from the inside out as she entered into its glow, one hopeful step at a time.

PENNY

Andrea stepped onto the fairway lit overhead by strings of bright lights and filled with children from all over the world, looks of pure delight spread over all their faces as the gate creaked shut behind her. Children with dark hair and dark eyes, and light hair with green eyes, and red hair with blue eyes, and every combination in between scurried in and out of shops. They ran through the fairway in saris and sweatpants, in burlap and blue jeans. Some wore outfits Andrea had only seen in pictures during social studies class, like they were from a different time period altogether. Girls in dresses with big red bows, and boys with shorts and socks pulled up almost to their knees. Some clothes were dirty, with stains and holes, others were bleach white and without a wrinkle. Many of the children held in their hands one kind or another of some delicious-looking treat.

A pipe from the roof of the candy shop pumped puffs of melting brown sugar into the Reverie air, reminding Andrea of how little she had eaten of her dinner and how badly she needed to get her hands on some food. Its warm sweetness lingered in the air like the final pages of a well-loved book. Reverie's binding, the near-invisible golden threads of magic, weaved in and through the tents and the shops and even the air, holding it together. Each shop, a page. Each tent, a chapter. The gates, Reverie's thick, protective cover. Andrea soaked in every detail, savoring it and carrying it deep inside her. Whatever Reverie was, it was a part of her now. And when she turned the final page on her time here, when she did finally wake up from whatever dream stuff Reverie was made of, it would be difficult for Andrea to leave.

"You're new here, aren't you?"

A girl who looked about Andrea's age skidded to a stop. She had on a cornflower-blue dress over a broad figure, shiny black-and-white dress shoes, strawberry hair pulled into pigtails, and a smattering of reddish-brown freckles across her full cheeks and the top of her nose. And she looked like she needed a nap. Deep purple circles formed the shape of a U underneath her eyes. Andrea knew those circles. She had seen them on her mom's face often since the divorce.

"Yeah," Andrea said. "How did you know?"

However tired this girl appeared, she definitely didn't act it. "For one, you've got that look on your face of *Oh my goodness, is this place real?!* Which makes complete sense, by the way. All kids make that face when they first get here. Sometimes *I* still make that face." The girl surveyed the scene like she owned the place. "Reverie is pretty amazing."

Andrea reached her hand in her pocket to hold on to the object inside it, though she couldn't quite remember why it was there in the first place. Or why she reached for it now. She nearly pulled it out to take a look, but the girl grabbed her wrist and squeezed it tight.

"I'm Penny. Penny Periwinkle." She stepped in close. "And I just have the most *amazing* feeling that we're going to be friends. I have a lot of friends here, of course, but I could always use another."

Andrea smiled. Something about Penny felt strangely familiar in this unfamiliar place. And it had been a while since anyone had been this excited to meet her. She had put off friendship the past few years, created distance between herself and the other kids. Read books during lunch and recess and looked up as little as possible.

Something pinched inside Andrea's heart at the thought. She knew she had done those things, but like the object in her pocket, the reason why escaped her. Maybe it was also hidden in that dusty corner she had given up for her ticket to get in, a side effect of forgetting. And if it was tied to the memory she surrendered to earn her ticket, it couldn't have been anything good.

"I'm Andrea Murphy."

Light rippled through Penny's tired, eager eyes. "Well, Andrea Murphy, get ready for the night of your life. And don't you worry about a thing. I know the ropes around here. I can show you the best tents, the best rides, the best food . . ."

Andrea's stomach chose that exact moment to rumble very loudly. She pulled her hands around it in an attempt to mask its groaning.

"Oh goodness, yes. You've come to the right place for a feast!" Penny yanked Andrea's arm, pulling her at a near run farther into the fairway and to a shop called *As You Wish Eatery*. She held up a finger for Andrea to wait and came back out with a tray piled with the kind of food a kid only dreams of being able to have.

"It's all delicious," Penny said. "But the shortbread cookies are my *favorite*."

Chocolate chip waffles with a mini mountain of whipped cream, shortbread cookies, french fries and a whole entire bowl of ketchup, a kebob of perfectly ripe strawberries dusted with snow-white sugar, ice cream with cinnamon stardust sprinkles. And *candy*. So much candy, including one of the lollipops Andrea had seen a sign for through the gate. Andrea stuffed her face, eating and eating until she knew her stomach would keep quiet for a good long while. So much better than Fake Family Dinner with its awkward silence and soggy carrots.

"Gee, you were really hungry!" Penny giggled. "Make sure you're in the clear of any hard objects with that one," she cautioned, pointing to the lollipop, her purple-lined eyes filled with mischief. "They make you dizzy. But it's super fun!"

The sucker, divided into two parts, a purple-pink top and a sunshine-yellow bottom, looked harmless enough. Andrea gave a tentative lick to the top, pausing to savor the sour sweetness of a raspberry kissed by the sun. Then, pursing her lips as the fresh-squeezed-lemon-tasting bottom coated her tongue. Her mind flashed to images of her grandma stirring lemon juice and sugar in a pitcher with a worn wooden spoon. It refreshed her like a perfect summer day.

The world in front of Andrea tilted, then straightened itself. She grinned and licked the lollipop again. Everything toppled, then spun in her vision, like she was riding a merry-go-round that turned so fast the scenery outside all smudged together.

She licked it one more time, letting her feet stumble as

they failed to find balance, as the lights and the shops turned to colored blurs. Penny squealed in glee somewhere next to her, or behind her, or something.

"Aren't they amazing?" Penny sidled up next to Andrea, holding her upright.

Light and breathless and *happy*, Andrea found a post to hold on to until her world stopped spinning. "It was great! I've got to tell Francis about this place."

"Who's Francis?"

"He's my little brother." Andrea scuffed the dirt with her sneaker, trying to ignore the twist of guilt that zinged near her heart. She wasn't sure why she'd feel guilt at mentioning his name . . . Maybe it was because she hadn't brought Francis in the first place? Something she'd have to make up for very soon, if she could help it. He'd experienced his own struggle when their parents split. She was sure Reverie would have a place for him, too.

Just then a tall, muscular boy weaved toward where Andrea and Penny stood.

"Oh, there's Miguel—he's one of my friends. Hola, Miguel!" Penny shouted. The boy glanced over at them but didn't stop or wave back. He continued on like he hadn't seen them at all and disappeared inside a shop a few doors down.

"Maybe he didn't recognize me," Penny said, almost to

herself, her eyes set on her shoes. "Golly, there's so many kids in here, sometimes it's hard to keep them straight."

Andrea narrowed her eyes, looking Penny over. Something about Penny's clothes, even some of the words she said, like *golly*, made her sound like someone from . . . well, not *now*.

Penny shook off the awkward encounter and beamed, revealing a small gap between her two front teeth. "You know what? I think it's time you visit your very first dream tent."

A surge of adrenaline pumped through Andrea, starting in her heart and working its way through her. The food had been amazing, but *this* was what she had come here for. To run away inside a dream. To forget her troubles, like the flyer had said.

Andrea grabbed hold of Penny's hand. Because whatever her trouble was, something gaping and endless with the pull of a black hole had, in this place, mercifully disappeared.

And it felt so good to forget.

UMBRELLAS AND DREAM CLOCKS

A giant clock tower stood in the middle of Reverie. Long, stretching lanes branched out from it in all directions like threads from a spiderweb, each lane lined with striped circus tents. A carousel spun near the tower, strung with huge lightbulbs and silver and blue flying horses bobbing up and down on golden rods. The sound of laughter and bold, brassy carnival music echoed out into Reverie's main square, bright like a scoop of orange sherbet.

Andrea's feet moved to the music of their own accord. *Step, step, back. Step, step, back.* Dance moves she had learned from her father a long time ago, in a life that was a million miles away.

Penny gestured broadly at the open plaza, her gaze lifted in pride. "Ta-da!"

A large full moon hung directly above the clock tower,

which was built from smooth blocks of shimmering stone. At the bottom of the tower stood a thick metal door with a giant lock. Above the door, in the same swirling print as all of Reverie's writing, was a sign labeled *Dream Bank*.

"What's the Dream Bank?" Andrea asked.

"It's where the Sandman keeps his sand—you know, the stuff they sprinkle over your eyes outside. To get your ticket. He keeps it locked in there. Wouldn't want a pack of kids throwing magic sleeping sand around."

Penny tugged Andrea forward and toward one of the lanes, tempting her with how much there was left to see, but Andrea slowed in front of the clock. The tower came to a single point at the top, and the face of the clock was different from anything Andrea had ever seen before.

Divided in two parts, the clock displayed a picture of a funny-looking old man in a nightcap with a sly smile. The top half of the clock said *Dreaming*, while the bottom half said *Awake*. A single hand poked straight out of the man's nose, its arrow pointing directly at the *D* of *Dreaming*.

"That's the Dream Clock." Penny released Andrea's hand. Both of them stared up at the tower, their necks bent as far as they would go. "And *that's* supposed to be a picture of the Sandman. He and his magical umbrella are in charge of all of Reverie. He's the ringmaster. And he's *very* powerful."

"The Sandman is real? I thought he was just a goofy legend."

"Oh, he's real." Penny shrugged. "But if you ask me, that picture isn't the strongest likeness."

"Why does he have an umbrella?"

Penny turned to Andrea, squinting her eyes into crescent moons. "The umbrella is *everything*. When you fell asleep in the hammock, your dream turned into a drawing, and that drawing tucked itself inside the Sandman's umbrella along with all the other dreams. And it became *real*. I know this because I know the Sandman . . . we're actually great friends . . . and he made me a special tent filled with my biggest wish in the entire world. And I saw how he did it. I watched his umbrella lift up in the air and spin and spin. The black key to the Dream Bank dangled down from the middle, still as could be in the midst of the rustle of thousands of twirling dreams. Oh, Andrea," she said, her voice soft and slow. "I hope you get the chance to see it."

Andrea hoped so, too. She stared hard at the man on the clock, imagining what it would be like to meet the man behind a circus built of dreams and his umbrella filled with drawings from the minds of the children who came to play.

"So does the clock tell us when our night here is over?"

"I think so," Penny said. "It hasn't moved since I got here. But, you know, time in dreams acts kind of weird."

That much was true. Andrea had been in dreams that felt

like hours but could only possibly have lasted a few seconds and others that felt like a few seconds but could have lasted most of the night. One thing was certain: Andrea wanted to experience as much of Reverie as she could before returning to the real world in the morning.

Andrea veered away from Penny as the force of one of the striped tents at the edge of a lane pulled her toward it, like she was one magnet and the tent was another. She stopped before the sign posted in silver paper that contained the tent's name.

Root River, with the picture of a shimmering willow above the words.

The tent beckoned her forward, billowing out and then retracting, matching its breath with her own.

"Nope!" Penny yanked Andrea's arm, breaking her focus. "Trust me, you aren't ready for that lane yet. And even when you are, you'll want to steer clear of this one." The girls stepped back into the warm light of the square and away from the *Root River* tent and its strange pull.

"But why?" Andrea asked.

"Never you mind at the moment, because *this* is how you pick a dream," Penny said. "Tell me, have you ever wanted to do something you never thought you'd get a chance to do in real life? Something that would require magic, or the impossible?"

They continued walking around the square, the draw of the *Root River* tent fading as Andrea sifted through all her childhood wishes: secret powers, unmatched skills, castles and hidden gardens and never-ending birthday parties, before latching on to the one that would make the best first escape.

"I've always thought it would be pretty cool to fly," Andrea said.

"Ohh!" Penny squealed. "Then I know exactly where to start! Follow me!"

They tore around groups of kids, many with the same sleep-starved circles under their eyes as Penny. As they ran past, Andrea caught a glimpse of her own reflection in a mirror sitting in the window of a crowded shop. Her face still looked normal, even though the mirror itself must have contained some sort of enchantment. In it, her normally blonde hair appeared endless, floating behind her in an invisible wind. She had always wanted longer hair. It was like the mirror read her mind and granted her wish, even if only for a moment.

They zoomed down a winding lane, past row upon row of glittering circus tents packed tightly together. So many dreams in one space. Each of them Andrea's for the choosing. The air hummed with anticipation, sending a rush straight through Andrea's veins.

Penny bent over and rested her hands on her knees, out

of breath, her cheeks flushed pink. "We're here," she huffed. "We're here."

Andrea stepped close to the canvas, stopping to read the tent's name. The sign contained a single word, *Soar*, and the image of a bird above it.

"This whole lane is filled with dreams that give kids powers they never could have in real life," Penny said. "And it's a spectacular place to start."

"Is it a good dream?" Andrea asked, remembering Margaret Grace's warning about nightmares.

"Oh yes." Penny's wet, purple-lined eyes shone. She squeezed her hands together in front of her chest. "It's almost perfect!"

Andrea approached the entrance slowly, wanting to savor the moment. The canvas fluttered open, flapping like striped butterfly wings in an unseen, unfelt wind. Glittering white contrasted against the deep indigo blue, attracting Andrea's eye, both standing out, bright and bold against the dirt ground, and blending in, a subtle, sparkling camouflage where it swept toward the night sky. Andrea reached out to it, tracing the back of her finger along the velvety fabric. Though staked into the earth, the tent quivered at her touch, delicate and tentative, questioning Andrea with invisible eyes. It pulsed with a gentle, quiet strength. Andrea pulled her hand back, slow and vigilant, as if one wrong move and it might up and fly away, disappearing from her sight forever. In the stillness, Andrea and the tents came to a quiet understanding. She promised to handle them with care. And the tents would let her stay.

"Are you ready?"

Andrea jumped as Penny's voice brought her back to the racket around her.

"You'll have to brace yourself when you enter," Penny continued. "It hits you fast."

"What hits you fast?" Andrea asked.

But before Penny could answer, a gust of wind blew past Andrea's face, stealing Penny's words as she opened the tent and leapt inside.

"Here we go," Andrea whispered to herself, her eyes and heart wide-open as she entered her first Reverie dream.

SOAR

A ndrea's lungs went from full of air to nearly flattened in milliseconds as the wind blew so hard in her face she couldn't refill them no matter where she turned her head. But any fear or trepidation faded fast as warm sunlight reflected off her . . . wings!

She had become a huge bird, with shining ruby-red wings that soared above the earth and soaked in the sun and warmed her to the core. Penny was blue, her wings the color of a pool on a hot summer day. But Penny's face was still the same. Still a girl. Still human.

This was unbelievable! But it was also right here in front of her eyes. Andrea could touch it, smell it, feel the magic pulsing through her. There was no way this dream could possibly be contained within the confines of a canvas tent. She wasn't looking at a dreamlike display. Or a creaky, artificial ride with bumpy wooden tracks. She had entered an entire world. And she was *flying* through it.

Penny swooped below Andrea, her wings a striking contrast to the muted tones of the earth below. She squealed, her voice half birdcall, half girl. "Isn't this the best?!"

Andrea's soul swelled, ballooning and stretching against her skin like a muscle long out of use but eager to regain its strength. Below them, a thick forest of trees went on for miles and miles, and above them, puffy cotton-ball clouds punctuated a sky that had begun to take on a hint of pink sunset. Even farther up, thin wisps of cloud hid the smallest sliver of moon Andrea had ever seen.

She turned upward, flapping her wings and slicing a cloud, thick as a well-kept secret, straight in half. She rolled the sharp taste of it, like a thin layer of salt, around on her tongue.

Penny pulled up beside her. "The only thing about this dream," she said, "is that we can't land. It's just a flying dream. The forest below is part of the scenery. But it's still amazing, huh?"

"It's great!" Andrea spun in a circle, cutting through several more clouds.

The excitement and wonder bubbled up and twirled inside her, building in her stomach and billowing out her chest, up through her throat, and exiting her body as a sound of boundless joy.

Laughter. It started small at first, a rough exhale. The joy gave way to more joy, so Andrea kept at it. Kept laughing, loud and free and almost as bright as the sun. Her laughter joined with the rays of light stretching down to the world below. Its luster grew into a song, raining droplets of music over the earth. Andrea hadn't laughed like that for such a long time. She had lost her laughter somewhere along the way, as she had so many, many other things. But this dream had worked its magic and swallowed up the loss, replacing it with lightness spilling over.

Andrea's heart constricted a little as ahead of them, a door appeared at the edge of a cloud. She slowed her wings, but still, the door opened up to a lane of Reverie tents as they approached.

"We can go in again!" Penny shouted. "Sometimes, I go in and out, in and out, in and out, over and over." She tucked her wings in close to her side. They transformed back into the arms of a girl as she slipped through the exit.

Andrea followed, stumbling briefly before pulling her fast-moving legs to a stop. She brushed a few stray feathers off her sleeve and watched them waft to the earth. Then, on second thought, she picked up one perfect, deep red feather and stuffed it into her pocket. There were already so many pieces of Reverie she wanted to remember, and this would definitely be one of her favorite chapters: the dream where she flew among the clouds.

She wanted to bring Francis back here, to give him a chance to laugh, too.

Andrea's heart pinched again, the guilt twirling behind it like a trail of smoke. Penny caught her wincing.

"Oh dear, are you all right?" she asked.

"I'm fine," Andrea touched her hand to her chest. "I think my heart is just beating too fast from the flying."

"Oh, well, if that's all it is . . . Once you recover . . ." Penny hopped up and down, unable to contain her excitement. "Would you like to try it again?"

Andrea waited for the feeling to fade, then looked back toward the center of Reverie, at the Dream Clock tower. The hand on the clock remained in the same place it was when she had first passed it by.

"Could we try a new one?" Andrea asked, her gaze still on the clock. "I don't want to miss *any* of the good dreams before my night is up." Having sunk her teeth into her first dream, Andrea couldn't wait to see what would happen next. The magical escape had jolted her with an energy she hadn't felt in who knew how long, and she itched to experience the next thrill as soon as possible. "What about an adventure?"

Penny grinned, lifting her eyebrows in delight. "Of course," she said. "Right this way."

PIRATES, STARS, AND NIGHTMARES

In the next tent they entered, *Buccaneer's Bounty,* Andrea's face met with a spray of salted sea and a sense of impending adventure. The crowded deck of a pirate ship groaned underneath their feet, and a pirate's black flag waved above their heads.

"This dream's quite popular," Penny said. "And this whole lane is filled with adventures just like it. I mean, who wouldn't want to find buried treasure?!"

The ship took a sudden lurch, and Andrea stumbled, losing her balance. A pirate caught her by the arm and set her upright, his hand cold as an ice cube on her skin. She rubbed her arm to bring back the heat.

"Careful there, matey," he said with a wink. "Wouldn't want ye to fall overboard. Thar's treasure up ahead!" He let go of

Andrea's arm and whistled a jaunty tune as he walked away.

Pirates of all sizes and shapes and colors, some with burly, knotted beards and others with peg legs and eye patches, stood about the ship, supervising pirate children who tugged on ropes and swabbed the deck and held long telescopes in front of their eyes. Each and every kid wore an expression that said they were having the time of their life, even the ones doing the scrubbing—Penny was right, this *was* a popular dream. The sea splashed on the deck at regular intervals, bringing with it relief from the heat of the sun.

"Land ho!" a boy with bronze skin and an orange, flowing wide-sleeved robe shouted. The entire crew shifted their gaze. Andrea craned her neck to get a better look. Ahead of them loomed an island covered in emerald-green trees with a single mountain peak so tall it touched the clouds.

The pirates barked orders at some of the children to "Man the sails!" and "Prepare to drop anchor!" Commands that the children were all too happy to obey.

Later, they exited the tent with breathless laughter, each clutching a gold coin after finding buried treasure on the beach with the dream pirate crew. The door to the exit had formed at the base of the mountain, and as much as Andrea would have liked to stay, there was still so much more to see before she ran out of time.

Andrea took an anxious peek at the Dream Clock, then broke out in a slow smile. The hand on the clock still hadn't moved forward. Which was perfect, because she was just getting started.

"It was cold, wasn't it? When the dream touched you?" Penny asked. "I saw you rubbing your arm."

Andrea nodded. "The pirate was colder than ice."

Penny smirked. "Took me a while to figure out all the dream stuff. I know the more popular the dream, the more solid it becomes. I've been in some where the dream figures are like ghosts. But it's not a hard-and-fast rule. I think sometimes the Sandman pours some bonus magic into the dreams he likes best to help the kids get a little extra from the experience." She shrugged. "I've heard stories that the Sandman can make dreams that are warm to the touch, but I've never experienced one. That might take some special magic, too. Most of them are cold, I think to help kids remember it's just a dream. A warm dream might make things confusing about whether or not it was real."

They passed by a stocky young boy with tawny skin and ruddy cheeks, beaming in front of a tent called *The Magician's Castle*.

"Some of the kids hang out by the tents they gave up for their ticket," Penny said, nodding to the boy. He politely nodded back, tipping the cap perched on his head. "Especially the popular ones. But some of the other ones, too."

Andrea stared at the eyes of the boy as they passed. They glimmered with pride above the deep purple crescents beneath. Maybe some kids liked to hang out by the tents they created, but Andrea would never count herself among them. Not in a million years. She couldn't remember what she had chosen to forget, but she knew she felt so much better now that it was gone.

The next tent they entered was called *Star Builder*, with the picture of a single hand and a star floating right above the name.

"Now," Penny said, "*this* whole lane of tents is filled with Reverie originals. Tents the Sandman set up to get Reverie started before the first child ever entered through the gates. They're wonderful and marvelous and built by magic as ancient as time."

"Wow," Andrea said, her skin tingling from the strange, thick energy thrumming through the entire lane.

Penny winked. "Just you wait, Andrea Murphy. Just you wait."

They stepped inside, and darkness surrounded Andrea like a blanket. A blinding blackness pervaded the entire space, darker than anything in a marker, or a painting, or even the night sky above her house. This was black like the universe before the dawn of creation. And silent as if there never before had existed a sound.

Above them descended transparent, twinkling, thin lengths of rope. Dozens, hundreds, thousands of them. Like strands of a spider's web with an added shimmer. They provided enough light now for Andrea to find Penny's face.

Penny tilted her chin toward the ropes and took a step forward. Andrea couldn't tell if a floor rested beneath her, but she didn't feel afraid. This dream felt like the breath someone holds as they wait for something wonderful to happen. The air around her hummed with potential, unbound by limitation.

Andrea ran her fingers along a few of the ropes. They tinkled like gentle wind chimes as they rubbed against her fingers and each other.

Above, a single voice sang out into the void:

And lo, the dawn of time.
And lo, let there be light.

A glowing being floated in the blackness above Andrea, Penny, and the twinkling ropes. Surrounded by and containing only light, it bore the vague shape of a person, though Andrea couldn't make out any specific features. This being was the source of the song.

Another being joined above. Then another, and another. They floated through the dark, collecting pieces of rope as they went. They zigged and zagged in a pattern, back and forth, left then right, over and under until the ropes formed a web in the shape of a star. It blinked and twinkled and pulsed with an energy Andrea could only interpret as an eagerness to be set free. One being held each point of the star, and they continued to sing:

And lo, the night has ended.
We sing the song of the dawn of day.
And lo, all of creation is good.

The beings lifted their arms, and at once the star floated up and away. Higher and higher, pulsing quicker and quicker, until it had shrunk to a small point and settled into its place in the sky.

The beings stared up in reverence for a moment before collecting more shining rope and twisting it into another star. They released it again, then made another, and another still. Their song rang out, and more and more beings joined them, forming stars faster and faster, their song resounding in joyful harmony like a chorus of angels. Maybe they *were* angels.

Penny leaned over. "Want to wish on one?" she whispered,

finally breaking the silence that had settled between them. "I always wish on one before I go."

Ahead of them in the blackness, the outline of a door shone with light all around its edges. It had been a long time since Andrea had wished on a star. It had been a long time since she had seen any point in trying.

"I'm okay," she whispered back. "You go ahead." For some reason Andrea couldn't quite put her finger on, something in life had taught her that wishing on stars didn't make wishes come true.

"Suit yourself." Penny squeezed her eyes shut, making a face like she had sucked on a sour lemon. When she opened her eyes, a single blinking bead of light floated in front of her face and began to rise upward and upward, until Andrea was pretty sure she saw it meet and join itself into one of the stars above their heads.

The door opened. It was time to go. Andrea took one last look at the beings and the stars, then walked through the door and out of the dream.

✳✳✳

Andrea blinked, her eyes adjusting to the bright Reverie lights before heading after Penny and turning down another lane. A cold wind blew past them and snaked around Andrea's skin, making her shiver.

They both jumped as a group of older kids piled out of a tent next to where Andrea and Penny stood, their harsh laughter ripping through the air. The tent they had exited was named *Jester's Playland*, with a picture of a clown at the top of the sign, smiling with cruel, wicked eyes.

"Can you believe that?!" a tall boy with black hair and olive skin shouted, slapping one of his friends on the back. "That knife looked so real."

"And the clown's laughter. Man, when I get home, I'm not going to sleep for *dayzz*."

The boys turned away from the tent, likely to seek out their next dreamlike thrill. As they did, Andrea's gaze landed on the back of one boy's green-and-white-striped polo shirt, the boy who mentioned the clown's knife. A jagged gash ran across it, the hanging fabric of the shirt flapping with each step.

Andrea froze. "Penny, what was that?"

Penny glanced up at the boy, observing the path of the knife across his back. Her eyes lit up, not with horror like Andrea expected, but with amusement. Like she thought it was funny. Like she was somehow on the verge of a laugh.

"Oh, that," she said, "is a Reverie nightmare." She jumped in front of Andrea, her purple-lined eyes teasing. "The lanes around here are all full of them. What do you think? Are you ready? Do you want to try one?"

Andrea pulled away from Penny. "Why in the world would I want to go in a nightmare?"

Penny side-eyed the jester's tent. "If you think about it, there's not really much of a difference between excitement and fear. Haven't you ever been to a haunted house? Or gone on a roller coaster? Same exact thing."

Andrea had been to a haunted house once. She had screamed and squealed and barricaded herself behind one of her classmates, hiding her face in the back of his shirt. Then, when they had made it through the horrors and found the exit, a sudden giddiness had overtaken her. Something she couldn't quite explain but that maybe came down to the fact that she was safe and the whole thing had been only pretend.

The feather and the coin in Andrea's pocket were enough to convince her that pieces of the dreams could stay with the people who went inside them, and Andrea wasn't convinced that going in a Reverie nightmare would be such simple fun. Walking willingly into a nightmare seemed a lot more like a trap than an escape, especially after what she had just seen with the boy and his shirt.

"You can think about it," Penny said, starting them down

another lane. "The nightmares can be pretty fun, if you're in the right mood for it. If you aren't afraid."

"I'm . . . not afraid," Andrea lied, glancing at the nightmare tents, which looked somehow darker and more sinister than all the others, their stripes leaning more black than blue. "I just don't know if I want to."

Penny caught hold of Andrea's wavering and took advantage, pulling her hands together in front of her face, mouthing silently: *Please please please please please please please.*

Andrea hesitated a moment more before giving in. "Fine," she said. Whether she wanted to or not, she trusted Penny's pleading, strangely familiar face. And Penny hadn't led her astray yet. "*One* nightmare. But not the clown one. I *hate* clowns."

Penny's face lit up like someone had flipped on a switch. "Good, because I think you'll regret it if you don't try as many things as possible. And I know where all the best ones are!"

Penny grasped Andrea's hand and walked her by a few nightmares, offering Andrea her choice. *Endless Ball* sounded tempting, but Andrea's mind flashed to the worst-case scenario. She imagined a bunch of people, trapped or cursed or something, who were doomed to continue dancing—long past when their shoes wore out, long past when exhaustion set in, stuck twirling and turning forever, their feet leaving bloody footprints on a once-shining marble floor. The thought of it made her chest so tight it was hard to breathe.

After walking the row back and forth a few times, Andrea settled on a tent named *Firefly Twilight*. The image of a simple firefly floated above the tent's name, and a crowd of kids gathered outside. It must be a popular tent, and Andrea had always liked fireflies. Even if it was a nightmare, how bad could it be?

THE FIRST NIGHTMARE

"This one only lets one kid in at a time." Penny nodded to the tent as they joined the line. "The door seals up until you've had time to get far enough along so the next kid won't catch you."

Andrea shivered at the thought of going into her first nightmare completely alone. But she didn't want to change her mind in front of all the other kids waiting, or for anyone to think she was scared.

"Don't worry. *I've* been in it before, lots of times. Once you're in, I'll run around and meet you at the exit. And this is very important to remember, Andrea: In every single dream, good or nightmare, there is always, *always* an exit. Some are easier to figure out than others, but you're never trapped. You just have to find the door."

Andrea nodded, only slightly reassured as they inched

closer to the canvas that sealed and reopened rhythmically, long enough to let a single child step inside, until she and Penny stood before the seam to the tent. Andrea glanced at Penny, who gave a nod and a smile as the tent unsealed.

Andrea took a deep breath and tried to look brave as she pushed aside the heavy canvas of her first Reverie nightmare.

The second the tent flaps shut, relief washed over her like a wave on the shores of a lake on a hot summer day. A pleasant, peaceful scene opened wide before her. Maybe Penny had been mistaken and this wasn't a nightmare after all, or maybe certain things were scary to some kids that weren't scary to others.

Andrea pinched her arm as a precaution and felt no pain, only the pull of skin between her fingers. Okay. She could do this. No matter what happened between now and the exit, this was certainly and only a dream.

A refreshing breeze wound through the otherwise still air, then twirled upward toward an amethyst sky. Tall grass tickled at the edges of Andrea's fingertips, and a rolling field lay out in front of her, dotted with dandelion puffs. Hundreds of fireflies winked slowly as they flew in lazy patterns above the grass.

Andrea waded into the field, the air thick with the scent of rich, damp wood and lush, ripe berries. A wooden table stood alone in front of her in the field, and on it sat a set of glass jars, fitted with lids with holes poked in the top. Perfect for catching fireflies.

Andrea tried to snatch a jar, but her body wouldn't move faster than the pace of the scene, a bit faster than slow motion, but not quite the speed of normal. Andrea brushed it off as one of the quirks of this dream and let her muscles relax, cupping her hands around the thick glass.

She held the jar open above her head and watched as a firefly looped around it, almost curious. She tipped the jar on its side and slid it around the bug's hovering frame, twisting the gold cap shut. Andrea brought her eyes in close to her prize. The firefly's light beat like a pulse as he rested on the jar's bottom. He stared at her curiously, with eyes more wise than bug-like. Andrea thought he might open his mouth and speak. But he just sat there with his light blinking, on and off, on and off, on and off, and his curious, curious eyes staring wide.

Andrea set the jar down, longing to see what it felt like to fall back onto the lush, long grass. She closed her eyes and spread out her arms, tipping backward, sinking into what could have been the softest pillow in the entire world. She opened her eyes and rolled back and forth, sending splashes of dandelion puffs into the slow-moving air.

A noise sounded to her right. Andrea sat up to find that another child had entered the slit of the tent. Her heart sunk a little. She didn't want to share this place with another kid. She wanted—*needed*—to be alone. It was time to move on.

Andrea stood and trudged forward through the grass until a set of hilly fields rose up to her left, with the lights of a warm-looking town at the very peak. Part of her wanted to climb the hill to explore the town, but something made her stop and watch. There were people moving slowly, only shadows in the near-dark sky, gathering by the cliff. Men in top hats and women with long-gowned silhouettes lined up right at the edge.

A woman in a ball gown walked toward Andrea from the darkness to her right, the swish of her dress matching the distant sound of waves hitting stone. Steely determination filled the woman's eyes, and her chin lifted in pride. She didn't speak, but somehow Andrea knew this woman's name. Her name was the Reaper.

The woman paused as she approached where Andrea stood, staring at her with a face white enough to belong to a ghost.

"Well, come along, child," she said, beckoning, reaching out a snow-white hand toward Andrea. "We must do what we must."

"I'm . . . I'm not sure what you mean." Andrea looked between the woman and the cliff, attempting to find anything that would clue her in as to what this nightmare had in store. "I don't belong here. I think you've made a mistake." She took a slow step backward and away. Something was wrong. Something was very wrong. Everything inside her screamed that she had to get away from this woman.

"There's been no mistake, *Andrea Murphy*. You are right where you belong. The sea witch requires a sacrifice, and tonight the honor is yours."

Andrea's forearms prickled and her stomach turned as her ears picked up on a low and eerie sound.

The shadowed faces of the townspeople turned toward her as they chanted something. Slow and quiet to start, but fast picking up in intensity and speed.

Her name.

She had to find the way out of this tent. *Now.* She spun away from the woman, searching, desperate to find that becoming a sacrifice to a sea witch wasn't the path to the exit.

Andrea pushed through the thick air as fast as she could until a slit of light appeared in the distance ahead, tucked inside a tree line. The shuffling of the woman's gown behind Andrea drew closer and closer.

"You must fulfill your destiny! You must fulfill your role!" the woman screeched, her voice shrill and cutting through the heavy air, her ice-cold fingers clawing at Andrea's waist and her warm breath hitting the back of Andrea's neck, making its hairs stand on end.

A fairytale cottage peeked out from the edge of the woods. Smoke piped out the chimney, and a warm yellow light shone through a small round window. The aroma of fresh-baked bread met Andrea's nose, calling to her, asking her to stop by the cottage for a visit. Tempting her to seek refuge inside its walls from the horror outside.

Margaret Grace's warning to not stay too long inside a nightmare still rang loud in Andrea's ears as she veered to the right of the cottage toward the tiny shaft of light. She stuck her hand through the slit. Cooler air met her fingertips on the other side. She pushed her body through the narrow opening, exiting the dream and finding herself once again in a row of Reverie tents.

Andrea doubled over, dizzy from pushing so hard through the heavy atmosphere inside the dream. She wiped sweat off her forehead with her sleeve, gasping with each breath, forcing air into her lungs while the desperate need to escape cloaked her like an ugly, worn, too-familiar sweater. The other dreams had filled her with wonder. This one, extreme and terrible as it was, filled her with an itching to run far away, something she had felt too often in her real life, though the reason why was tucked away in a circus tent somewhere as part of what she had chosen to forget. A lot of good pinching had done her. The dream had seemed so real there hadn't been any space in her brain to remember it was pretend. She would have to do a better job of keeping her wits about her in the future.

"So?"

Andrea looked up and into Penny's gleeful face.

"How was it?!"

Andrea settled back into the lane, landed her gaze on the striped blue and white of the tents, tapped the packed dirt beneath her feet with her shoes, and inhaled the enticing aromas brushing past the air beneath her nose. She caught hold of the laughter and movement of the other Reverie children and released a huge breath, letting every ounce of tension melt away like hot caramel over a waxy red apple on a stick.

Then, despite herself, she smiled.

She was fine.

Penny's goofy *I told you so* face dissolved into laughter, and Andrea joined her.

The nightmare was better than anything scary in her own life because Andrea could enter and exit the nightmare tents knowing that none of it was real. *She* was in charge, for once, of when the horror ended, and she couldn't wait for the next thrill.

Andrea pulled Penny into a massive hug, and they spun

and twirled and giggled together in the middle of the Reverie lane.

Wait.

Andrea tore away with a sudden jerk, the breath snatched clear out of her lungs.

It had been such a long time since Andrea had gotten swept away in a moment with another person. There was a reason she couldn't lose herself like this, even if she couldn't remember what the reason was.

She had to stay in control.

Or someone was bound to get hurt.

SOMETHING AWFUL

"**A**re you okay?" Penny leaned over Andrea's bent frame and placed a hand on her back.

"Yeah, I just . . ." Andrea stared at the ground and focused on breathing in and out, in and out. "I . . . I think so." She caught her breath and stood back up. She tried to shake off the fear of letting her guard down, and plastered an attempt at a reassuring expression on her face. "Come on," she said. "I'm sure there's so much more to see."

The two girls walked in awkward silence for a few minutes before Penny cleared her throat, concern seeping through her forced-casual tone. "So, obviously, as your friend . . . I'm curious what brought you to Reverie tonight. What's your story, Andrea Murphy?"

"My story?" Andrea kicked her dirt-stained sneaker into the ground, trying to ignore the bristle she felt inside her at

Penny's use of the word *friend*. "What's *your* story?" Maybe if she could deflect the question, she wouldn't have to deal with things she didn't want to answer, or couldn't remember in the first place.

"Mmm, nope," Penny insisted. "I asked you first. And it's okay, I promise I won't tell a soul. A friend doesn't tell another friend's secrets, even if they're big."

Andrea took a step back. She had no idea why Penny needed to know anything about her at all. If Francis were here with her instead of Penny, he would understand. The divorce had wrecked him almost as much as it had wrecked her. She'd have to come back with Francis a different night. He would be much better company.

Andrea winced as the twist of guilt around her heart returned again, stronger this time. She brought her hand to her chest and pressed it, willing it to go away.

Something was wrong.

"Like . . ." Penny continued, for once oblivious to Andrea's discomfort. "Why did Reverie show up for you? Every kid who comes here has a story. Something hard or sad in their real life that they want to get away from for a while."

"My life's fine." The twinge faded and heat rose through Andrea's cheeks as she repeated the same lie she had told so many people ever since her parents split up. Since her life started coming apart at the seams. When whatever caused that heavy, lingering sadness came rolling in. When her teacher caught her zoning out during class, staring out the window with empty eyes. Or when her mom tried to make ridiculous fake-happy conversation during breakfast. As she sat against the cold brick wall at recess, watching other kids play. *I'm fine. I'm fine. I'm fine.* It was the lie she had used to hide the cracks and holes inside her heart. It was the lie she told herself, hoping that if she said it enough, it would one day come true.

She had told the lie so many times, but she couldn't remember why it existed. It was something that happened *after* the divorce. Her reason for coming to Reverie in the first place, the thing she had chosen to forget. But she couldn't seem to shake the ripples even here, surrounded by Reverie's colorful distractions. The sadness was still there, hovering on the edges. And so was the armor she had built in order to cope.

Did the other kids who came to Reverie still feel the after-shocks of whatever had shaken up their lives so much they were desperate to escape? Or was Andrea the only one? Was this how Reverie was supposed to work—being haunted by the ghost of what you chose to leave behind?

Maybe something was broken. Maybe *she* was too broken for Reverie to fix.

Penny looked at Andrea closely. "Friends tell each other the truth." She narrowed her eyes. "And I don't believe you. Reverie doesn't come to kids whose lives are *fine*."

"You don't have to believe me." Andrea shrugged, shoving a hand into her pocket and curling her fingers around the item tucked inside it. "But I promise I'm okay. My life's okay. Maybe Reverie made an exception, because I just came here to have some fun," Andrea said, anger flaring up at Penny for bringing up such a sore subject, making her words loose and sharp. "And I never asked for a friend."

"Oh." Penny's face fell. "I see."

Andrea bit the inside of her cheek. Her hard heart ached for Penny, who had been nothing but nice to her, but not enough to take back what she had said. She had to protect herself. She couldn't let her armor fall.

Most people never questioned Andrea's response. In fact, most people looked relieved when Andrea told them she was fine. Like saying she was fine somehow gave them permission to believe it was the truth. And here was Penny, a near-complete stranger, acting like she saw straight through Andrea's façade.

Maybe it was time to take a break from Penny. Andrea liked it better when people believed her. Or at least pretended they did. She peeked up the lane and toward the Dream Clock, which still stood frozen, exactly the same as it had been when she arrived.

"Oh." A wave of disappointment washed over Penny's face, as if she read the thoughts inside Andrea's head. "You're going to leave me now, aren't you?"

"No, I'm—"

"Don't worry," she said, forcing a smile. "I know that impatient peek at the Dream Clock. I'm used to it. Most people let me show them around for a bit and then go their own way. I'll just meet up with one of my other friends. They're all over the place. And maybe I'll see you here again one of these nights, if we ever choose to return."

Guilt churned inside Andrea's gut at Penny's kindness. She smacked her heel into the ground but couldn't bring herself to respond. The guilt . . . it felt so familiar. *Too* familiar. She had felt this guilt before, not only now with Penny, but every single time she thought of her brother since she'd arrived.

Your fault. Your fault. Your fault.

Andrea pulled away, doubling over as the weight of those words threatened to pull her under.

"Hey, are you okay?" Penny reached a hand out, but Andrea brushed her off, giving a small nod and trying to ignore the swirling in her heart as she stumbled down the lane and away from Penny.

Andrea's forehead broke out in fine beads of sweat as the dark shadows at the edges of her mind crowded close, and the voice she knew too well growled again from deep inside.

Your fault. Your fault. Your fault.

She was guilty. Of lying to Penny for sure. But of so much more as well.

She had given something up. She had left something behind. She had chosen to forget a great and terrible sadness, but her brain itched to remember. And now it wouldn't let her go.

What horrible thing could she have done?

"Andrea, please let me help you!"

"Leave me alone!" Andrea snapped back, stumbling farther down the lane and clutching at her chest, which had grown as heavy as if it were weighted down with bricks. "I'm not feeling well . . . I have to go."

She turned quickly around a corner, trying not to feel even more guilty about the fact that Penny stood there, looking worried, still as a statue in a crowd of people where everyone else had found a friend.

Andrea took another step forward, and the world in front of her blurred like it had when she licked the magic lollipop. The tents melted in front of her eyes. They formed shining, striped puddles of slime that wound their way into the lane and toward the place where she stood.

She had chosen to forget something awful, and now her heart was trying to remember.

None of the other children noticed. They kept running and laughing and moving about as if the entire world wasn't dissolving around them. Only Andrea watched as the other children and their faces shifted into blobs of color, melting and joining the river of dreams. The Dream Clock, still fixed on *Dreaming*, began to chime, unrelenting and thunderous in Andrea's head. She tried to run away from the current headed straight for her but slipped, losing her footing on the oily ground. She slapped her hands into the dirt to stop herself from a bad fall just as the melted dream world pooled around her feet.

RALPH'S THRIFT SHOP

Andrea startled awake on the floor of her room, her head pressed into the gray star pillow. Harsh morning light from the window hit her face, along with the repetitive beeps of a truck backing up outside.

She still wore the jeans and T-shirt she had been wearing the previous night. She must have fallen asleep instead of slipping out into the garage.

But, man, had she had a weird dream.

Reverie. Penny. Its magical circus tents. She had been certain it was real. A wave of disappointment rushed through her, sinking her stomach. The end of the dream had been bad, but most of it—the beauty, the wonder, the magic—had been so, *so* good.

And it had been all in her head.

Andrea walked to the window, blinking slowly. The room was empty. Francis must have already gone downstairs.

A white truck that read *Ralph's Thrift Shop* was parked in front of the yard, the back open, the ramp pulled down. Her dad's car sat in the driveway along with a stack of boxes. Her mom stood on the grass, her robe wrapped tightly around her, her arms folded across her chest.

Andrea walked down the stairs and out the front door.

"What's going on?" she asked. She figured that the man, who must be Ralph, was probably picking up a bunch of items her mom had intended to sell at the garage sale she could never organize herself enough to have. But that wouldn't explain why her dad was here, too.

He carried another box out of the garage and set it on the driveway. Ralph picked it up and carried it to the truck.

The sun briefly flickered before Andrea, like a lightbulb threatening to go out. Her mother turned to Andrea with tired eyes brimming with tears that wouldn't quite fall.

"We told you last night, sweetie. It's time to let go of Francis's things."

Andrea's blood grew hot. "What? Why? Where is he?" Andrea marched to the garage, searching wildly for his mop of sand-colored hair. "Francis?"

Her father froze, a fresh box cradled in his hands. "Andrea, this isn't the time."

"The time for what? Where is my brother?!" Andrea's

body pumped with heat. Her skin burned like she was on fire. She hated how they looked at her. Her mom, her dad, Ralph from *Ralph's* stupid thrift shop.

Her parents shot each other a look that said: *What am I supposed to do with her?*

Andrea clenched her fists and tensed her arms, certain if she yelled loudly enough her brother would hear her. That he would come running and explain what was going on. Why they were putting his things on the back of a truck.

"FRANCIS!!!" Her words tore through the air as she yelled his name one, two, ten more times until she had scratched her voice raw and tasted iron at the back of her throat.

Ralph stared, a mix of pity and confusion on his round, red-cheeked face. He pulled out his phone, checking the time, then walked back to the boxes and picked up another—

—like heck he was going to drive away with Francis's things.

Anger raging through her, Andrea ran full speed toward the man, smacking the box out of his hands and spilling it open all over the grass next to the drive. She fell to the ground and pulled together the fallen items, scooping them into her arms and nestling them close. Hoping that by holding them near her, she'd be able to figure out *why* her brother's things were being taken.

The box that had spilled contained all of Francis's precious items. The things he displayed proudly on his dresser. Andrea had caught him, on more than one occasion, rearranging his valuables, trying to get the perfect effect.

There was his Batman figurine and some plastic dinosaurs. An empty mason jar. A shining, smooth brown stone they had picked up at the gift shop in a museum. And pictures. So many pictures of their family all together: standing in front of the swing set with Francis after their father spent the whole day putting it together; smiling up from a dining table filled with platters of food and a steaming turkey; sitting around a Christmas tree, with wrapping paper strewn all over the floor; and a selfie of the family at story time, snuggled on their parents' bed, days before they split.

"He's gone," her mother said, kneeling on the earth next to her daughter, her face streaked with tears. She smoothed down Andrea's straggly hair in pressured, repetitive motions and kissed the top of her head. "He's been gone for three years. Andrea, I'm so sorry, but you can't do this. It's time to let go."

Tension flooded from Andrea's body as she leaned into the softness of her mother's chest, inhaling the faint floral notes of her perfume with each shaky, shallow breath. *In and out, in and out.* Andrea's mind slowed after a few moments, small spaces forming between her frenzied thoughts.

The bright sun slipped behind a cloud, erasing Andrea's shadow. And there, in the silent beat between breaths, she remembered.

The flyers taped all over town. The news stories. The phone calls from horrible people pretending to know where he was.

Family dinners with two empty seats at the table most nights. Her father's. *And Francis's.* Christmases with fewer gifts under the tree. An empty lower bunk. The endless hours Andrea had spent alone. *Brotherless.*

She had lost her shadow.

Francis was gone.

Andrea doubled over, the remembering sucker punching her in the gut, making her fragile heart shudder. She wrenched herself away from her mom's embrace and crawled back to the box, confusion weighing her down, pushing her toward the earth.

"Francis!" the world flickered again as she screamed, over and over again, pulling more and more of the items from the box into her arms, each muscle in her body stiff as wood, fighting against each and every attempt to bend.

He was gone, but she couldn't remember how it had happened. The life with Francis and the life without him felt like the beginning and the ending of a story that was missing its middle.

She clutched the empty mason jar as the entire world around her stopped moving, like she had pressed the pause button on her life. A single mosquito hovered, frozen midair, inches in front of Andrea's face.

She had wanted to forget what happened the night he disappeared. And inside the gates of Reverie, she had. But if Reverie was only a dream, why would she still not be able to remember that night now that she was awake?

Andrea let Francis's items fall to the ground with clanks and clashes as she fished inside her pocket and set the world to moving again. The sun reappeared and reflected off the glass from one of the pictures, sending searing light into Andrea's eyes. Three objects met her hungry fingers. Andrea pulled them out and held them in her open palm.

A soft bright red feather. A smooth golden coin. And the trinket she had kept for such a long time: a small yet weighty vial of shimmering sand. Sand exactly like Margaret Grace had used to put her to sleep after she rode her bike off into the woods and arrived at Reverie's gates. Where she pinched herself and learned that Reverie was *real*.

And if it was real, Reverie couldn't have been something she had only dreamt last night. It had to be a place she had actually been. Maybe it was still there, waiting for her, out in the abandoned field. Maybe she could escape there now.

Andrea didn't want to think anymore. Didn't want to remember anymore. She wanted to go back to when the sharp edges of the past softened and she hid herself away in a world built of dreams. She was sure she wouldn't mess it up this time. She would let the sweet release of escape and forgetfulness take over. She'd run from tent to tent and never stop. She'd run so fast the pain couldn't catch her.

She *needed* to go back.

So there on the ground, with her mom and her dad and Ralph staring at her in pity like she was some sort of lost puppy, Andrea tucked the feather and the coin back into her pocket. She opened the vial of sand and poured a bit into her palm. She closed her eyes, sprinkled the sand over them, and said the words that had taken her away from all this horror in the first place.

"I ask the Sandman to take me away, to a land of dreams in which I can play."

"Andrea, what are you doing?" her mother asked, her voice coming from far away, like she spoke to Andrea across a great distance.

"I ask the Sandman to take me away, to a land of dreams in which I can play."

The ground beneath her began to tilt. Hope leapt up in Andrea's heart.

"I ask the Sandman to take me away, to a land of dreams in which I can play."

The smell of fresh-popped corn curled beneath Andrea's nose.

ROOT RIVER

Around Andrea the feet and legs of children scuffled, and above her towered the blue-and-white-striped Reverie tents. Her skin brushed not against the soft, manicured grass of her front yard but the packed dirt of Reverie's lanes in the exact place the dream world had melted around her.

Andrea stood up, dusting the dirt off her jeans and grinning from ear to ear, pure elation washing away all the desperate sorrow.

She pinched herself, welcoming the sting.

Reverie was real. And she was back.

Andrea tucked the vial of sand back into her pocket. She needed to get inside another dream. Good dream, nightmare, she didn't care. She needed to be swept away. This was why she had come here in the first place: to forget that Francis had disappeared, and how.

Andrea ran into the first tent she could find at the edge of the square that didn't have a bunch of kids standing around it.

Here it was again, like it had been waiting for her, its pull just as strong as it had been the first time.

Root River.

Penny's warning played like a loud recording in her mind, and Andrea recognized this lane as one of the ones Penny said was full of nightmares, but how bad could any dream or nightmare in this place really be? And it was clear the dream itself *wanted* her to enter.

Andrea pulled the canvas open and rushed inside it.

She entered into a park scene drenched in moonlight, with trim cut grass and a border of trees. A bubbling brook curved a path between her and a large playground on the other side. A willow tree stood by the river, its wispy leaves urging her forward, nearer to the water. She set her toes next to the river's edge. Up close, a stronger current ran through it than she had been able to see from a few yards back. Clear water at the top dissolved into blackness so deep she couldn't see the bottom. Still, something about the willow felt kind and gentle, like an old grandfather tree used to guiding children across the busy waters. She reached forward to brush the leaves with her fingers, trusting the old tree would wrap itself around her and lead her safely across the rumbling stream.

Andrea squinted, catching the curved lines of an ancient face etched into the tree bark. Deep grooves ran up and down over the tree's wide, lumpy trunk, and a scar carved horizontally across it like a ragged scowl. Past the willow stood the playground, haloed by a single floodlight. The iron chains of a lone swing creaked forward and back, the only movement in a sea of still.

Damp, heavy air seeped around the place where Andrea stood. The scene sat strangely inside her, like a faint memory. Like she should know what would happen next. Like she had been here before. She reached down deep in her mind, probing it for more. Slowly, the pieces flooded back to her: a park, a river, a tree pretending to be kind. A fall. Legs turning to stone.

Andrea took a step back, her breaths growing ragged and shallow. She had heard of this place before—through her brother's panicked, whispered words during the years he woke up from his recurring dream.

No. Not his dream. His *nightmare*.

The willow dragged me down into the water, he had said. *It turned me into stone.*

Andrea filled her lungs with as much air as she could in the moment before the willow plunged her underwater. Its branches wrapped around her arms and legs, digging deep and sending slivers beneath her skin. The roots of the willow curled around her ankles, dragging her to the bottom of the river.

She stretched her fingers, grasping for the surface, for anything to hold on to. *Nothing.* Freezing water slammed against her chest. She kicked wildly toward the surface, hoping she had enough time left to fight her way free.

The crisping started in her toes, stiffening them and moving quickly through her ankles. Her legs grew cold and numb and hard and smooth. Like stone.

Andrea opened her mouth to scream as metallic river water rushed deep into her lungs. She smacked her face, pinched at her arms. Flailed her working limbs, churning plumes of mud into the already murky water. She twisted, wild and unblinking, in every direction for the door that would let her back out into the safety of a Reverie lane. Penny had said there would always be a door.

Finally, when her lungs burned, and a blackness started edging into the corners of her vision, and her muscles had tired, and the moon's pale glow wrapped softly around her, and her hair floated in lazy tentacles slowly toward the surface, Andrea saw it. Directly below her, a small slip of light reflected off a door handle on the river's bottom. With her last ounce of strength Andrea pushed her arms down to it and pulled the door open, heavy under a layer of thick, slimy mud. She used her grip on the handle to yank herself and her lower half, now completely turned to stone, down through the exit. Her pulse quickened as her fingers touched dry air just past the boundary of the tent, and then as her arm and upper body followed.

One massive push later, and Andrea landed on the ground in front of the wretched tent, drenched, spitting out water and gasping for oxygen. The water soaked into the dirt around her, creating a muddy, blob-shaped shadow.

A group of kids, each under the influence of a dizzying sucker by the look of it, stumbled past her, almost running her over, before snickering and wandering away farther down the lane.

Andrea lay back, filling her lungs with the crisp night air.

She had been in Francis's dream. Andrea tossed the idea around in her oxygen-starved head as long as it took to stick. *She had been in Francis's dream.* And if she had been in his dream, that meant her brother had, at least at some point, been to Reverie. The Sandman, whoever he was, collected kids' dreams as the price of admission. Francis must have paid with his nightmare to get his ticket, choosing to get it out of his head and into a Reverie tent.

Andrea wrung out her hair and stood tall, shaking off any

lingering drips and not caring that her clothes were now cold and wet. She had to figure out when her brother had been here. If anyone had seen him.

And if, somehow, he was still here.

RIPPLES

"I was worried about you." Penny appeared out of nowhere, tapping her foot on the ground and crossing her arms, her eyebrows lifted and lips pursed like she had been waiting a long time for Andrea to exit the tent. "Hope you enjoyed almost drowning. I warned you to steer clear of this one."

"I'm *sorry*." Andrea crossed her own arms, uneasy about Penny's random appearance and her *I told you so* tone. But as much as she hated to admit it, Andrea was also relieved to see her. She softened her stance and her voice. "This might sound crazy, but this nightmare is my brother's dream."

"Why would that sound crazy? Lots of kids come to Reverie."

Andrea bit the inside of her cheek. As freaked-out as she was, she could also use some help. So she told Penny her story—that Francis had disappeared, and how long he had been gone. She would have told her more, but there was so much Andrea still couldn't remember.

Penny's face eased as Andrea spoke, the same sadness passing over her expression as it did every time someone learned what had happened. Then the sadness, like always, melted into pity.

"You gave up a memory, didn't you?" Penny asked. "To earn your ticket?"

Andrea scuffed the dirt. "How did you know?"

"You can't remember your whole story. The kids who give up a memory have ripples . . . all the memories attached to what they gave up get lost as well. Unless you decide to remember. I wouldn't have asked you so many questions if I had known you gave up a memory." Penny held her hands out in front of her in warning. "Please, don't try too hard to fill in the holes on your own without going through your tent. Strange things happen when a kid tries to do that . . . strange, confusing things."

Andrea didn't say anything, but she was pretty sure she had already broken that rule and found out what happens, what with Reverie melting around her and waking up to the nightmare back at home.

"I'm so sorry," Penny said, her voice wobbling like she

might burst into tears any second. "If you gave up a memory, it must have been immensely painful. Don't you just cry all the time?"

"Nope." The truth was that Andrea hadn't cried in a long while. Before, when Francis had first disappeared, Andrea was pretty sure she would bleed tears. That her tears could form a river, a sea, an ocean. That once she started crying, she would never, ever be able to stop. So, on a windy fall day when the leaves covered the ground like a blanket and the rain washed away the ink on the posters with her brother's face, she chose never to cry again.

Penny placed her hands on her hips and paced in front of the tent. "I don't think Reverie follows the regular rules about how it fits into time, since the kids here seem to be from all different years," she said. "But if you read the ticket, it's only good for one night. I'm certain that even if your brother was here three years ago, he wouldn't be with the group of us here now. His night would have been over. He would have gone back home . . ." She paused. "Are you quite sure it was Francis's dream?"

Penny set a tentative hand on Andrea's shoulder and spoke to her like a parent speaks to a young child. "I mean, it's possible someone else had a similar nightmare. It might not have been his."

91

Andrea shook her off. She didn't like people talking to her like she was made of glass, and she didn't appreciate being brushed off so quickly, especially by someone who claimed to be a friend.

"Okay, fine, jeepers," Penny lifted her hands in surrender. "I'm only trying to help." She paused, looking up at the black sky.

A pack of kids carrying a bunch of helium balloons depicting the image of the Sandman with his light blue cap and pajamas barreled past.

"Maybe I should ask him."

"What?" Penny followed Andrea's eyes to the children and the balloons as they disappeared around a corner.

"I said," Andrea repeated, louder, "maybe I should ask the Sandman if Francis has been here."

"Oh no," Penny said, holding up her hands in protest. "I know the Sandman, of course. He comes out to see me *all* the time. But kids aren't supposed to bother him. He spends a lot of his time alone. He is *not* to be disturbed."

Andrea didn't really care about Penny's word of warning. If he ran this entire place, if he watched over everything, then he must know which children entered and if Francis had been here at any point. "Do you know where I can find him?"

"Of course I do," Penny crossed her arms in front of her chest once more, a scowl on her face. "I told you, I know almost everything about this place, and the Sandman and I are *great* friends. He's almost always in his dream tent that he made for himself. It's in the lane straight behind the Dream Clock. It's bigger than the rest of the tents and is striped black and white instead of blue. But you shouldn't do what you're thinking."

"If you know him so well, why don't you come with me? How mad could he be if his *friend* brought someone to him in need of his help?"

"I can't," Penny shook her head. "He won't like you if you do it," she murmured, her voice at nearly a whisper. "He's not to be disturbed."

Andrea set her jaw. What was Penny's problem? If the man who created Reverie couldn't stand to help a girl in search of her brother, what kind of place was this? And why was Penny so scared when finding Francis was at stake?

Andrea didn't have time to deal with Penny's fears. She turned away from Penny and took off toward the Dream Clock tower, kicking dried soil behind her dirty sneakers as she went.

"He won't like you!" Penny yelled after Andrea as she pulled away. "You'll ruin everything for yourself if he doesn't like you! Just you wait and see!"

"I'm sorry!" Andrea shouted back. "I've been waiting three years! I have to try!"

Something had grabbed hold of Andrea, taking over every

thought, something small and steady and swelling inside her.

Hope. That the man in the cap and pajamas would have the answers to her questions. That maybe there was still a chance to find her brother.

Andrea continued to run, pumping her arms so fast the friction from rubbing against her shirt burned and her clothes grew dry. Another twinge of guilt turned inside her for leaving Penny behind in the dirt again, even for disappearing on her parents on the lawn in front of their house.

But she had to stay focused. Couldn't let the guilt come back to haunt her and risk Reverie melting around her once more, leaving her stuck and confused in a world to which she wasn't ready to return.

If Francis was here, or had been before . . . if that really had been his dream, then she'd have a new clue that might help her find him. One way or another, Andrea wouldn't let anything distract her until she found out.

THE SANDMAN'S PRIVATE DREAM

Andrea craned her neck to take in all of the Sandman's tent. It wasn't a single circus tent with one point like all the others: Formed out of multiple tents and sweeping points, each striped ink-black and snow-white with tiny sparkles, the Sandman's dream stood tall with one massive tent in the middle, larger and higher than all the rest. The tents glistened in the reflection of the moon, which still hung directly above Reverie's Dream Clock.

This lane was quieter than the others, and less populated. Only the occasional child skittered by, possibly because the Sandman's tent took up most of the lane. There weren't as many dreams to enter here compared to the others.

A thin layer of fog floated above the ground, creeping around the massive structure. Andrea reached her hand out to touch the canvas, then drew back like it had stung her. This tent felt different from the rest. More solid. Heavier. Which maybe made sense, because the images she had seen of the Sandman were of an old man. Maybe the dreams of young children were lighter. Perhaps dreams got heavier as people aged.

The low fog swirled around Andrea, curling upward, almost like a finger, inviting her forward. The answers she sought were inside. She knew it. She only had to enter to find them.

Andrea swallowed and looked once more at the full, round moon before venturing into the darkness of the Sandman's private dream.

***

Women's perfume, sadness, loss, unfulfilled wishes. Andrea stepped into a small room painted with pink and gold vertical stripes that smelled of all these things. In the center hung a gaudy gold chandelier dripping with tear-shaped crystals.

A dusty, long pink chair stood alone on one side of the room with a tattered blanket resting across it, unfolded. A pink dresser with gold handles sat alone against another wall. On it stood a single photograph in a frame. Andrea went to it, bending over and peering into the eyes of the person in the photo. The black-and-white image of a girl with dark, thick, curly hair stared back at Andrea, her wide eyes amused at something behind the camera that Andrea couldn't see.

Andrea knew this girl. It was Margaret Grace. The girl with the sand and the tickets outside Reverie's gates.

In the wall opposite the entrance stood a painted gold door. There was nothing else in the room, no windows, no other pictures or art.

Andrea took hold of the door handle and entered the next part of the dream.

Raucous adult laughter greeted her from an adjacent room at the base of a stairway in a house that felt small but fancy. The scent of beef stew wafted toward her from a nearby kitchen, and a little girl sat on a step and played with a wooden stick that had a cup attached to the top. A ball dangled from a string connected to its base, and the girl moved the toy in swooping motions, trying to catch the ball inside the cup.

Andrea stepped toward the girl, the wooden floor creaking under her feet. The girl's eyes jolted up to meet her, lit up first with excitement, then shaded over quickly with annoyance.

"Who are you?" The girl stood, placing her hands on her hips. "You aren't my brother."

Andrea stared into the girl's face. She was younger here,

maybe five, six at the oldest. But it was definitely Margaret Grace.

Andrea shook her head without speaking.

"I'm waiting for my brother," Margaret Grace continued, glaring.

"I'm sorry," Andrea said, the hairs on her forearms rising. "I'm not sure where he is." This place had too many missing brothers.

Margaret Grace stomped her feet in frustration. Then she screamed, loud and high and shrill, and ran up the stairs, disappearing down a hall. The adults in the adjacent room grew quiet, and Andrea felt their eyes on her, even though she couldn't see them. She felt their judgment, like she, too, wasn't whom they expected to see.

Andrea turned down a hall lined with doors, each punctuated by a heavy doorknob in the shape of an S. She twisted one of the handles, the door opening to another part of the dream. Andrea quietly exhaled in relief, eager to escape the angry, unseen eyes.

She now stood in a long, dimly lit hall that felt as if someone had left it only moments ago, and smelled like dust and her grandfather's breath after a post-dinner drink. The walls here were painted forest green on top and lined with panels of deep mahogany wood on the bottom. Andrea's feet clicked on the floor, echoing down the hall like she wore boots or heels, even though she still wore her sneakers. Another one of this dream's strange, enchanted tricks.

The walls were packed tight with pictures of Margaret Grace. In some, she was laughing, casting side-eyes at the camera, her face filling the frame. There she was, in another, about the same age as the girl at the gate, giving a kiss on the cheek to a lanky boy in patched-up clothes and slicked-back hair who stood proudly beside her. Then a picture of her again, a little bit older, about Andrea's age, in a marvelous ball gown, standing at the base of the stairs Andrea had just passed by, one hand placed daintily on the railing.

The pictures and the hallway ended at yet another door, made also of mahogany wood, and with a coal-black round handle.

Andrea clutched the handle, popped the door open, then walked through it. It closed behind her, silent and fast, leaving her completely in the dark.

She jiggled the handle in an attempt to go back the way she'd come, but like Margaret Grace had said, there was no going backward in a dream. Andrea's discomfort only grew as darkness and air thick enough to choke her clutched at her body from all angles. She had reached the center. She knew it by the heaviness alone. By the sadness. Like this tent had a gravitational pull and everything else in the dream orbited around it.

Something in the dense air shifted. A cool breeze cut through, making the room buzz with invisible anticipation.

Andrea jumped as the room sprung to life. A dozen or so sets of strung lightbulbs swung up to the tip of the tent, humming with primitive electricity. Opera lights framed a broad stage, casting their glow in a spotlight on a deep pink velvety curtain.

Andrea thought for a moment that she might be alone, until she saw the silhouette of the man in the front row, facing the stage.

A silhouette so different from what she had expected. This was no bald grandpa in cute pajamas. No, this silhouette bore broad, tall shoulders, and a top hat perched on his head.

Gooseflesh prickled up Andrea's arms. Penny's warning didn't seem so silly now that she was this close to the Sandman. She had invaded his private dream. She understood that now. All of this, each part of his dream, felt so intimate compared to the other dreams she had been in. All these potent memories wrapped up inside one tent.

She tried to push away the nerves, because none of it mattered, really. She couldn't go back. Even if the Sandman didn't appreciate her company, even if he kicked her out of

Reverie as a result, she had come here for a reason. She wasn't giving up on the chance to find out about her brother, not when she was this close.

The same fog from outside wound its lazy way around the rows of empty seats, unfurling onto the vacant stage. Andrea crept through the rows, clutching the backs of the chairs to keep herself oriented in the cloud until she stopped directly behind the man. The fog thickened around her and around the man in the top hat as well.

Andrea squared her shoulders, ready for whatever this encounter would hold.

"Excuse m—"

"Shhh," he interrupted, cutting her off. He stood, the silhouette of a man melting away into a real person through the curls of smoke. Shadows still covered his face. He towered over Andrea in a crisp, gray tuxedo, made of fabric with a hint of sparkle. He held a gray umbrella in front of him like a cane, and his plum velvet top hat glistened through the fog.

He lifted his angular chin, looking down at Andrea as she got a first glimpse at the Sandman's olive skin, distinctive nose, slicked-back salt-and-pepper hair, and the same dark purple circles under his eyes that so many of the Reverie children had. At the corner of his eyes, a few rays of wrinkles spread toward his ears, thin as cracks in fine china. He looked nothing like the picture on the Dream Clock and in Reverie's cartoonish souvenirs. He was so much younger than Andrea had imagined. A man, but not an old man. Not even close.

The Sandman placed a long finger over his lips. "We'll get acquainted when she's finished." A guttural sound, almost like a giggle, bubbled upward from his throat as his mouth curved into a strange, expectant smile. "You're just in time for the show."

A PERFECT WISH

The Sandman offered Andrea a seat next to him in the front row. Andrea wasn't too sure she wanted to see the show, whatever it was, but if he wouldn't talk to her now, she would have to wait. She slid into a spot a few seats down. The Sandman sat and fixed his eyes on the stage.

As if on cue, the curtains pulled aside and Margaret Grace stepped forward, exactly the same as in the final photograph in the hall and smiling with closed lips at the nonexistent crowd. Built out of stardust and silver, her sleeveless gown sparkled from every possible angle, bold enough to catch the eye but gentle enough as to not be blinding. Margaret Grace gave a soft curtsy and then began to sing.

Piercingly clear, satiny smooth, and as full as an ocean, Andrea had never heard a voice like hers before. If her voice were a color, it would have been the orange of the last sliver of sun before it slipped beyond the horizon. Within the first few notes, Andrea almost fell under her spell and forgot why she had come in the first place.

Almost. But she could feel the dream's pull, its attempt to hypnotize her brain, to dull it to everything except the dream sequence itself. She had come to ask the Sandman a very important question about her brother—if he had been to Reverie. But the longer she stayed here listening to Margaret Grace's song, the less important it seemed. The draw and the distraction didn't feel too different from the other dream tents she had been in, except that in the others, she hadn't been trying to remember something important. Andrea worked to stay focused, to not let it slip away.

The Sandman sat, still and unblinking, while he watched Margaret Grace sing. He loved her very much, that was easy for Andrea to see. But his shoulders slunk forward, and his brows pulled together in pain. She knew that face. In fact, she had made that same face herself when looking at family pictures with Francis still in them. She had once stopped and stared for so long that her mom shouted her name five times in a row just to snap her out of it.

Staring at the Sandman now, she wondered what could have happened to make him look at Margaret Grace that way.

Margaret Grace's song swelled to a peak and then ended

softly on one held-out, haunting note. When it was over, the air that was only a moment ago filled with sound got swallowed in the vacuum of silence. Smoke billowed into the room as the Sandman jumped to his feet and clapped and whooped and stomped a standing ovation.

"Brava!" he shouted, his hands wrapped around his mouth. "Bra-va!"

Margaret Grace surveyed the imaginary roaring crowd with an expression of gratitude, but also something else. Something more serious. The face you make when you are saying goodbye. She glided backward then, and the curtain closed before her.

The Sandman's clapping slowed to a stop. He turned to Andrea, wiping away a few diamond-like tears from his eyes.

"Pardon me," he said. "But it never fails to move me. That was my Margaret's final show."

"Her final show?" Andrea asked. "I'm sorry, sir, I don't understand."

The Sandman heaved a deep and heavy sigh. "She's . . ." He shook his head in near-disbelief. "She's gone."

"But I met her outside when I got my ticket. She was a bit younger, but . . ."

"Younger . . ." he said, his voice soft, his eyes glazed over like his mind had gone somewhere far away. After a long moment, the Sandman shook his head, regaining clarity. He bent over and peered into Andrea's face. "Quite right, you did meet her. Only not in the way you might think. But there's time for all that. You must be new. And since you are in my tent, you must already know who I am." The Sandman held out his arms in a sweeping showman's gesture. "I am the Sandman." He lowered his arms and softened his voice. "Now, tell me, child, who are you?"

"Andrea?" Andrea said, more a question than an answer.

"Welcome to Reverie, Andrea." The Sandman smiled. He set his umbrella once more in front of him, resting both hands on top. "How can I help you?"

Andrea wasn't sure if the Sandman was truly happy to see her or if he was being polite, but she had to hope he really did want to help her. If he didn't, he wouldn't have bothered to ask.

She shifted her weight, trying to grab the fringes of her question for him from the fog inside her mind. She had come to ask him something *very* important. "Well, sir . . ."

"One moment." The Sandman held out a hand in front of Andrea's face. "We will talk as we stroll. I could use some fresh air. Check in on my lovely dreamers." The door to the dream appeared on the side of the tent, an opening in the canvas much like the entry.

Andrea hoped she'd remember what she needed to ask him once they got out in the clear night air.

The Sandman picked up a brisk pace once they exited the tent, forcing Andrea to take almost two steps to his one long stride in order to keep up.

"This," he whapped the side of a tent, "is a wonderful dream. Have you been in it?"

Andrea shook her head and read the name on the sign: *Bubble Delight.*

"You enter, and you're wrapped up inside a bubble! You float around bouncing into the other children, who are each in their own bubble. Up and down and bouncy-bouncy. Ha!" His laughter cut through the air like a sword. "Delightful indeed!"

They walked like this for a while, the Sandman pointing out tents, tipping his hat to the children as they passed. At one point, Andrea turned behind her to find that they had collected a river of children, an entourage of dreamers. The Sandman continued on with a sly smile, taking pride in his following. Like he was some Pied Piper who had been play- ing the flute the entire time they walked through Reverie's lanes.

The Sandman slowed as they arrived at Reverie's Dream Clock, where a show had set itself up in the square. The performers wore the colors of flames and juggled fire sticks and launched themselves in choreographed movements into the sky from a set of strategically placed trampolines. They flipped and twirled around the fire one after the other in a hypnotizing rhythm against the darkness of the sky. Herds of children paused in the square to watch them, their purple-lined eyes open wide in wonder.

"From time to time, I release one of Reverie's dreams into the square," the Sandman whispered. "That way all the children can enjoy it at the same time. Isn't it something?!"

Andrea nodded. She had had no idea the dreams could be freed from their tents.

"The heartbeat of Reverie," he said, his voice hushed in reverence.

Andrea looked up at the Sandman. He wasn't staring at the show, like she would have guessed. Instead, he gazed in awe at the Dream Clock tower.

"It doesn't look much like you," Andrea said, referring to the image on the clock and stalling for time. She feared the Sandman would get distracted or bored and walk away from her before she had a chance to remember her question. She needed to focus. She rubbed her eyes, trying to clear her head of the lingering fog that she suspected was caused by being so close to the source of Reverie's magic.

The Sandman chuckled. "I suppose he does not. But, dear child, what are dreams if not filled with contradictions?"

Andrea looked between the picture of the Sandman on the clock—the wrinkled old man with the kind face and the nightgown and cap—and the Sandman next to her. A man of precise movement and tall posture and commanding presence. The ringmaster of a circus built of dreams. The one who might hold the answer to her question, if only she could remember it.

"Mr. Sandman . . ." she whispered. "I have something I need to ask you."

The Sandman ripped his gaze from the clock tower and stared down at Andrea with a gentle smile. "Of course. Come this way." He formed his fingers into a pair of scissors and made a cutting motion through the air behind him. The children who had followed them stayed in their places, their eyes fixed on the show, while Andrea and the Sandman strolled along the edge of the square.

They passed by several tents at the entrance to different lanes, *Sleigh Ride*, *Spring's Eternal Bloom*, *The Gray Nothing*, and finally, at the entrance to a lane of nightmares, *Root River*. Andrea paused in front of it. She ran her fingers along the name. She had been in this tent before.

The memory came back to her then like she had sniffed

smelling salts. The water rushing into her lungs, the roots wrapping around her ankles, her legs turning to stone.

Her question.

Francis.

The Sandman stopped and tipped his head, waiting for Andrea to speak.

The words poured out of Andrea, forceful and fast like a fire hydrant without its lid. "My brother, Francis Murphy. He went missing. And I went through the dream that he used to have . . . this nightmare. Right here. And, well," she let out a shaky breath. "Do you know if he's been here? And when? I need to find him."

A flicker of sadness passed over the Sandman's face. "Ah," he said, his voice somber. "I see."

He lowered one knee to the earth so his eyes were level with Andrea's and tucked his umbrella underneath his arm. "Dear child," he said. "So many, many children enter through Reverie's gates. There's no way I could possibly know them all." He folded his hands and placed them on the top of his knee. "I *am* very sorry."

"Oh," Andrea pulled her lips to the side, unsure what to do next. A dry heat spread behind her eyes, and a black emptiness settled inside her stomach. His answer had been so . . . short, and so vacant of any of the things she wanted to hear.

She had known finding the Sandman might not lead her to her brother directly, but she hadn't expected it to be a dead end.

"Chin up," the Sandman said. "Even though I can't tell you if your brother was here, there is still a way I can help."

Andrea pinched her eyebrows together. "There is?"

"Of course there is. Come along. Follow me." He pushed himself to standing and ducked into a quiet lane.

Andrea followed in silence, at a much slower pace than before, until they reached a place in the lane between two tents that was empty, save for a few blades of brown, dry, overgrown field grass quivering in a quiet breeze.

"Before I make you my offer," the Sandman said, stopping in front of the vacant space, "you must tell me two things. First, how long has your brother been gone?"

"He disappeared three years ago."

"Oh dear," the Sandman said, almost at a whisper. "Thank you for telling me that. And second . . . I must know . . . some children come to Reverie to remember. And others, well, they come to Reverie to forget. I must know, Andrea, which one are you?"

Andrea wasn't sure what he meant by the question. Her confusion must have been evident on her face, because the Sandman tried a different angle.

"Did you give up a dream you wanted to live in over and

over again and remember? Or did you give something up so it would be out of your head? So you could forget?"

"Oh," Andrea said, scraping against the dirt with the toe of her shoe. "I paid with something I wanted to forget."

There it was again, the small twisting of a hand inside her, digging around in a dark corner, trying to find the piece she had lost.

"I think it was what happened the night my brother disappeared." Andrea took a deep breath in and let it out slowly. "I think it was somehow my fault."

The Sandman's thin lips pulled into an even thinner line. "Oh, my child," he said. "I'm so, so sorry. I understand your pain more than you know."

Andrea sniffed and looked to the side. "Thank you." She blinked back the burning that used to turn into wetness and fall down her face as tears. "I came here to forget, and I did forget . . . but I still felt guilty—I guess I still *do*—so I tried to remember on my own, without going through my memory tent. Then things got really strange and I went home for a little while. When I came back I found my brother's nightmare."

The Sandman nodded. "Let me tell you something useful."

Both man and child turned to face the Dream Clock, where it peeked out above the endless sweeping tents and the flags that waved at the top. "The Dream Clock is vital to Reverie's existence."

"I know, the dream sand." Andrea had been through this with Penny, and already at the square with him.

"Ha! Indeed!" The Sandman punctuated the end of the sentence by lifting his gray umbrella up above his head and slamming it, tip down, into the dirt. "But this—this simple, wondrous umbrella—contains all of Reverie's dreams."

He knelt down to Andrea's level once more. "And each dream a child gives up to enter is imprinted here, inside my umbrella on a piece of parchment, which is then built into one of Reverie's tents, or released into Reverie's world if I will it to be so."

The scent of mystery and twilight and secrets whispered in the dark wove around Andrea, infused into the threads of magic in the Reverie air.

"But we must not spend our lives chasing shadows. Your brother has been missing for three years, dear child. That is a long time for a person to go missing, and to have him ever return home."

The Sandman sounded too much like her parents had when the police stopped searching for Francis. Andrea looked away, the heat behind her eyes growing even hotter.

"No, no!" The Sandman held out a hand. "No need to

despair. You see, I want all the Reverie children to be happy. And I offer each child who seeks to find me the *exact same reward*." He reached in his pocket and pulled out a piece of folded parchment. He handed it to Andrea, then pulled out a small stick of charcoal as well. "I offer you a *wish*, Andrea. A perfect wish tent built just for you. It doesn't have to be a dream you've already had, or a nightmare, or a memory. It can be something special that has never before existed in the history of the universe, something made out of a wish from your heart. Something that is only yours."

Andrea could hardly believe it. Penny couldn't have been more wrong about what happened to kids who sought out the Sandman. She was so sure it would bring trouble, that the Sandman wouldn't like Andrea, and here he was, offering her a gift.

"Your pain is so great," he continued. "You wear it around you like a shroud. It's time to release yourself from its burden." He took the tip of his umbrella and tilted Andrea's chin up so she would look him in the eyes. "If you wish, I can build you a tent to make the pain disappear. I can build you a tent to *truly* forget it all."

Forget.

It had been such a relief to lose the memory of the night Francis disappeared. She had so enjoyed Reverie's tents, feeling lighter than she had in years while tucked away inside them. Then the whole experience had morphed into a living nightmare when she woke up at home and had to relearn he was gone. Her return to Reverie had brought with it another round of momentary reprieve until she'd entered Francis's dream. Andrea craved that relief again, craved the forgetting. So strong was her need for it that it brought her body to aching.

Forget. Forget. Forget.

The Sandman looked at her, his eyes soft at the edges. He watched her, neither as a ringmaster nor as a salesman, but as someone who understood the desperation inside her. Someone who had felt it himself.

"Your tent," Andrea said. "Did you build it as your own perfect wish?"

The Sandman nodded.

"The woman in the tent, and at the beginning of the dream, and at Reverie's gates. She's your sister."

The Sandman cleared his throat. "Yes, she is, in a way. My sister . . . she—she used to come here with me when we were children. And she . . ." He hesitated, frowning and lowering his eyes. "She died very young. So I created a tent filled with my Margaret in all her favorite places, in all the ways I knew her best. You see, I am in Reverie to remember."

Andrea tilted her head, considering what it would be like if she asked the Sandman to build her a tent with a dream version of Francis. She didn't much like the thought. Maybe that was what the Sandman had meant, about her being there to forget.

"Wouldn't it be better," the Sandman continued, "if there was a tent just for you where all memory of Francis, of all your pain, would be wiped away? Where the family of three eating dinner behind the panes of the dining room window would be just that. A family of three." He leaned in closer, tempting her to put the charcoal to the paper. "You'd never have to leave the tent, if you so choose. What relief it could offer. It might be exactly what you need."

Andrea felt the gravitational pull of the Sandman and his magic umbrella, felt her mind slowly letting go. She was so tired. Of the sadness, and the guilt, and the pain.

She closed her eyes and exhaled softly, imagining a scene of her family where her parents were still together. Where she never had a brother. Where she never felt the missing of him. And where she never had to protect her heart from breaking because there was never any threat of danger or pain.

She opened her eyes and stared at the parchment.

Forget, forget, forget.

Andrea twirled the piece of charcoal slowly between her

fingers. It left a smudgy black stain wherever it met her skin.

"All you have to do is draw it," the Sandman said, his voice slow and low and even. "And you can stay, and forget, and be happy."

Andrea knelt next to the Sandman on the ground and moved the charcoal closer to the paper. *Yes.* It would be a big, beautiful house, and her mother, and her father, and none of the sad things and all of the good.

But wait.

Andrea's hand hovered, barely floating above the parchment. Parchment thick and yellowed and curled at the edges like the poster for Reverie attached to the tree in the moonlit woods. Her insides twisted again, stronger now, winding her up tight like a spinning top, ready to unfurl.

There was no way to create a perfect wish and keep all of the good and also erase Francis. Because *so much* of the good revolved around him. Quiet moments at the kitchen counter, a box of crayons shared between them. His saggy bathing suit as he ran through the spray of a sprinkler while a golden sun set on a hot summer day. His scrunched-up face and unrestrained laughter as Andrea dressed his little body up in their father's clothes.

Andrea shook her head, like it had filled itself in with cobwebs over the past few minutes and she needed to knock them down. Goosebumps ran up her arms at the thought of what she had almost done. She had wanted to forget her pain, not forget Francis entirely. Maybe the two were far more entangled than she once had thought.

She needed to find out what had happened, even if all she learned was that Francis had been to Reverie a long time ago. The loss of her brother had come with so many questions, and now, here, she had a chance to finally get one small answer. She would solve nothing by forgetting she had a brother. In fact, by wrapping herself in a lie, even one disguised as a beautiful dream, she would lose what little good remained. Living in a dream where she couldn't remember Francis didn't mean that in the real world he hadn't still disappeared.

If the Sandman didn't have the answers she needed, Andrea would have to go looking for them on her own.

Andrea dropped the black stick of charcoal into the dirt and sat back on her heels. "I'm sorry," she said. "I'm not sure what wish I want yet."

The Sandman snatched up the charcoal and tossed it in the air, catching it with his other hand. Andrea picked up the parchment and they both stood.

"How about this," he said, his voice kind and soothing, but with a hint of tension in the back of his throat. Andrea recognized it as the voice she had used to talk to her brother when she had tried to get him to do something she wanted but knew she'd have to be clever. "How about I leave you with the paper and the charcoal, and when you're ready, you go ahead and draw your perfect wish. Bring it to me, and I'll make it exist for you. Does that sound all right?"

Andrea nodded, but inside her head, a different plan was forming. She would look for clues around and in her brother's nightmare. She would ask all the Reverie children she could find if they had seen him. It was possible some of them had come multiple nights; maybe someone would remember.

She was so lost in thought, she almost didn't notice the charcoal the Sandman held out toward her between his long fingers.

"Thank you," she said. She didn't know what tent she would ask him to make, if she asked him to make anything at all, but she was glad to have the opportunity to make a wise choice when she was ready. She grabbed the charcoal and stuffed the parchment in her empty pocket.

The Sandman tipped his hat and continued down the lane, picking up another following of children in his wake, chin held high, surveying his land of dreams.

Andrea turned back to the nightmare tent that she was certain had belonged to Francis, hoping to find a clue.

For the *just in case* that hummed inside her.

For the prickle of hope that what had broken could be fixed and that the burden of guilt she carried might be lifted off her shoulders.

For her lost little brother and the sliver of hope that he was out there, somewhere, still able to be found.

THE BOY IN RED-AND-BLUE-STRIPED PAJAMAS

The lanes were quieter than normal as the show continued on in front of the Dream Clock tower. Andrea shuffled through the dewy-eyed crowd of Reverie children as another dream, composed of a single male performer wearing a glittery midnight-blue bodysuit and face paint to match spun with a vacant expression from a long stretch of black cloth that somehow hung from the sky. He moved, fluid and silent, inside and outside and through the frame of a floating metal box. The performer twisted and walked through the air and suspended himself by his ankles from the fabric, arching his back and twirling slowly, every muscle poised to precision: arms open, delicate blue fingers splayed, toes pointed, face empty. Silver glitter fell like a gentle snowfall from the air above, dusting the heads of the children who stood below.

Andrea peeled her reluctant eyes away from yet another hypnotic component to this land of dreams; she was no longer here to be entertained. She was here to learn all she could about her brother and his nightmare and how and when he had been to Reverie. And if she could get some of those questions answered, if they left her with even the slightest clue, then she was determined to try to find Francis.

She approached the *Root River* tent and ran her fingers once more along its shimmering sign.

"Francis," Andrea said to herself. "How did you find your way to this place?"

She waited a moment, wondering if she should go back through the dream to try to find some answers, though she didn't move yet. Her legs still remembered the heavy feeling of turning into stone, and her throat still burned from the water rushing inside her.

But she knew she had to go in; this was her only new connection to her brother. Unless her desperate mind was attaching someone else's dream to him . . .

A shuffling sounded from behind the tent. Andrea turned with a jerk and followed the noise to where the backs of two tents met between the lamplit lanes.

"Hello?" she called.

Silence answered. There weren't any other children in sight. Maybe she had heard a scampering mouse rather than a person.

Then again, maybe it *was* a person. A person hiding. Andrea tried to shut down the thought, but it didn't work. The thought grew, quiet but persistent, gaining volume inside her head.

Maybe it's him. Maybe it's him. Maybe it's him.

Andrea's breath froze as she listened for another noise through the silence. Her palms broke out in a sweat, and she tried to wipe the cool slickness away on her jeans, to no avail. If it was Francis's dream, maybe Penny was right. Maybe he came back here night after night and hung out around the tent that had gained him his admission. Maybe he felt bad that so many kids got sucked into his nightmare. It would be very like Francis to worry about the other kids and to want to warn them away.

There.

Andrea heard another shuffle and turned just fast enough to see a boy, about age six, with sandy-blond hair and her brother's red-and-blue-striped pajamas disappear around a corner.

"Francis!" Andrea bolted after the boy, scrambling farther down the nightmare lane, which was packed with striped tents, each containing a strange and terrifying world inside it. Children spilled into the lane from the square, where the show must have ended. Andrea looked to the left and to the right, trying to catch a glimpse of the boy through the weaving crowds. Her chest tightened. If it really was her brother, why was he running away?

A frenzy of children from preschoolers to teens, from wide to lanky, dressed in everything from hoop skirts to filthy rags and polished black shoes to bare feet, moved through, talking and bumping into Andrea and laughing. They created too much movement to keep anything straight. Andrea's stomach sank as she feared she had lost him.

"Francis!" Andrea called one more time out of pure desperation, her voice harsh and grating above the happy crowd.

She lurched as she caught another peek of the boy, ducking into a tent only a short way ahead. She sprinted to catch up, first glancing, then pausing at the sign at the front of the tent.

The Frigid Place.

Still breathing heavy, Andrea noticed the image of a snowflake above the sign. She didn't want to go into another nightmare. But if that boy was Francis, if he was *here*, then even if he hid himself away in a dream that was in fact filled with terrible, awful things, Andrea had to go inside it. She was desperate. She would do anything if it meant a chance to find him.

Andrea pulled open the edges of the tent, and a frosty

gust of air chilled her through her clothes. Francis knew she hated being out in the cold. Whoever this boy was, he had placed a bet she wouldn't follow him in there.

He bet wrong.

She entered, and her breath hitched the second she inhaled the freezing air. She stuttered her breathing, in and out in ragged, broken bits while icy fingers nipped at every exposed inch of her skin.

Andrea drew her arms around herself in a useless attempt to get warm and blinked as her eyes struggled to adjust to the unforgiving white of a vicious, near-blinding blizzard. She didn't like the thought of Francis in this place. Wandering in a world of ice. The air in the tent felt cold enough to cause frost-bite in minutes at most. Little pinpricks danced all over her skin, and Andrea moved forward through a snowdrift, even though she could no longer feel her feet.

Tiny icicles formed on her eyelids and off the tips of her fingers as she pulled her heavy feet through the snow. In a merciful break from the wind, a tall, dark object came into focus only a short way ahead.

A coat rack. Loaded down with a half dozen heavy fur coats and, below them, animal-skin boots.

Andrea rushed as fast as her frozen fingers would go to slide the large boots over her sneakers, which were now as good as ice cubes, and wrap herself in the coat's warmth. The minute she did, her brain began to thaw. The coat melted her like butter in a microwave, like a steaming cup of cocoa in hands that had just played in the snow. This was better. She could trudge forward like this. She could keep looking for the boy she hoped was her brother.

One step at a time, Andrea plodded deeper into the winter storm. Mountain peaks framed her path, and in a few minutes she caught the trail of some nearly snowed-over footprints, small enough to belong to a kid. She caught glimpses of the boy up ahead though the breaks in the snowdrifts, between biting swirls of white.

"Francis! *Francis!*" Andrea yelled to him, her voice echoing through the ravine, fully aware she could be calling out the wrong child's name, but desperate enough not to care. Every so often the boy looked back, his blurred, pale face framed by rosy cheeks and ears tinged with pink. He, too, wore a child-sized fur coat. But the farther she went, the clearer it became that this boy still didn't want her to catch him.

At last, the blizzard stopped and fell to a stillness, quiet as death except for the crunch of snow under her feet. Andrea stood on the edge of a frozen lake so smooth it could have been glass. Out of breath, she puffed out thin clouds that dissipated before her eyes.

Andrea squinted. There he was, almost to the other side of the lake, shuffling his legs across the slick ice. But now, he was no longer alone.

A tall man with a gray coat and tails that flowed like a cape walked beside him. A gray umbrella swung from the man's left hand in between the moments he leaned on it to take a long stride. On his head sat a plum top hat.

The Sandman.

The Sandman had lied.

He put his arm around the boy, patting him twice. The kind of pat you give a kid who does a good job at something. Who does as he is told.

She wanted to yell out again, but the boy and the Sandman exited the dream through a door carved into an ice mountain on the far side of the lake. The Sandman flicked his umbrella open, then closed, almost too fast for Andrea to see, and then he disappeared.

She moved to follow them, but the world of the dream morphed before her eyes. The sky above her lightened, brighter and brighter until Andrea could barely keep her eyes open.

Don't stay too long in a nightmare. Margaret Grace's words of warning rang loudly between Andrea's ears.

Maybe the clock for this dream had started when the

Sandman and the boy entered and she had been too far behind when the dream was supposed to end. Or maybe the Sandman had sped things up with that flick of his umbrella, a cruel trick to keep her from catching someone he didn't want her to find.

Andrea bolted for the exit, but it was too late. Her feet slipped while the sky fell around her like jagged pieces of a puzzle, sizzling into ash as they hit the ice. She fell twice, breaking her fall with her arms as her body slammed into the unforgiving glassy lake. The fur elbow of her left sleeve ripped open, and the skin beneath it screamed. She wasn't going to make it.

The light extended further into the dream, scooping up the mountain peaks and the snowdrifts, making its way to where Andrea lay flattened on the lake, creating clouds of ice crystals with each wasted breath.

The bright light wrapped itself tightly around her, squeezing her from every angle until she was sure she would break.

THE FRIGID PLACE

Andrea gasped awake.

In her bed. In her room. Under her twisted blanket. She ran a clammy hand over her heated forehead, one thought repeating itself over and over again inside her mind:

It was a dream.

It was a dream.

It was a dream.

Andrea could feel her fingers and wiggle her toes. Relief pulsed through her with each warm surge of blood through her veins. She swung her legs over the side of the bunk and hopped down, wrapping her blue blanket around herself and heading to the door.

That was when she saw it.

It was early autumn. The weather cooling down after a long, hot summer. Winter was on its way, but it hadn't arrived.

Yet narrow, jagged fingers of frost crawled all the way up her window.

Andrea opened her bedroom door, stumbling backward as chunks of a snowdrift from the hall crumbled into her room.

Don't stay too long in a nightmare.

Either she had stayed too long or the Sandman had pulled a trick of time. Andrea hadn't understood what Margaret Grace—or the dream that was Margaret Grace—meant when she said it, but each time she had broken a Reverie rule she had ended up back at home. And this time *The Frigid Place* had crawled its way out of her head and into her bedroom.

Terror curled inside her as Andrea reached under her bed for her shoes. She felt it in the jolt of nerves running through her veins and the eerie silence throbbing its endless nothing through her ears. There was no telling what she would find downstairs, but Andrea couldn't stay in her room forever. She needed to find out the boundaries of the nightmare's reach, if it had claimed more of her home than her bedroom window and hall.

Andrea took a deep breath, exhaling visibly in the polar air, and trudged through the hall and down the stairs, heading straight for the kitchen. Icicles hung from every doorframe and frost crept up the walls, in some places digging deep into newly formed cracks in the plaster.

When she saw the kitchen she stopped: There stood her parents, their bodies unmoving and their faces grayish blue. Andrea forced her way through more snow with fury, pausing in front of her father, whose hand hovered a few inches above the counter and clutched a black pen.

Andrea leaned close to him, sticking a finger under his nostrils, checking to see if he was alive, if he was somehow breathing in this chilled state. But everything was still. His clothes were too stiff to move, and the expression on his face was pulled tight, strained, like he had looked in the weeks after Francis disappeared.

Except for his eyes. The lids were frozen open, but the eyes themselves were wet. Moving. *Alive.* They followed her as she leaned from side to side, filled with all the pleading he couldn't get his mouth to speak. Pleading for Andrea to help him.

Andrea's skin crawled at the sight, guilt once again coursing through her. Here was her dad, silently pleading for her to help him, and she didn't know *how.* She pulled back as her own eyes threatened to betray her, building up that hot, burning feeling she worked so hard to hide away.

Beneath his hand rested a piece of paper and handwriting she'd recognize anywhere. As the words went on, they grew jagged, like her father was still trying to write them as his hand began to freeze.

ANDREA, WHERE ARE YOU???

Andrea reached out to touch him, but she might as well have stuck her hand in the ice bin in the freezer.

This was all her fault. She had done this to them. In her eagerness to run away, she'd made her parents fear they had lost not one but *two* children. She had made their real-life nightmare come true for the second time. And then she had frozen them.

"Dad," she shook her head and set her jaw. "I'm so sorry. I was only trying to help. I was trying to bring Francis home. But don't worry, I'm going to fix this." Andrea's legs wobbled like they might buckle underneath her at any second. She hoped her voice sounded more confident than her mind and body felt.

Her father was trapped in a nightmare, all because of her. All because she had entered Reverie. Because she wanted one moment in time when she could forget, and then because she wanted to bring Francis home. She was trying to *make things better*, and all she'd done was make them worse.

But it didn't make any of the words she spoke now less true. She was going to fix this. She could set all this right. She just had to figure out how.

Andrea's mother was equally bad. Her eyes at least were frozen closed, mid-blink, but her eyeballs moved behind them, grating against the ice coating her lids. She was bent, hunched over a pot of coffee, an empty cup on the counter beside her.

The entire house groaned around Andrea under the pull of the ice and the weight of the snow, threatening to collapse and crush them. An avalanche made of snow and wood, ice and drywall, frost and shingles, and deadly dreams.

"I . . . I have to go and find help," she said, hoping her parents could still hear. Andrea slid open the porch door and stepped into the world outside.

For some reason, she had expected the freeze to be contained to her home. To be able to knock on a neighbor's door whose grass was still green and ask to use their phone. She would call the police and the ambulance and the fire department. Whoever she could think of that would come and help. They would search Reverie for Francis. Then they'd chase the Sandman's dream circus straight out of town.

But none of it mattered because the entire world outside was frozen, too.

Bare branches glistened in the harsh sun, each encased in a glaze of ice. The houses as far as Andrea could see were all wrapped in the same degree of winter, maybe with people inside them exactly like her parents. Frozen.

Had her mistake somehow turned the entire world to ice?

Andrea hadn't agreed to this when she entered. She had agreed to escape, not to have nightmares follow her home.

There was too much at work here trying to prevent her from learning the identity of the boy she had seen.

There could only be one reason for that: The boy *had* to be Francis. She was certain now.

She was also certain the Sandman had lied, and that he was going to great lengths to keep them apart.

Andrea let out a scream that echoed throughout the silent, empty air. None of this was okay. None of this was right. She hated feeling trapped. Hated the sting of deception—that there existed a person out there who thought it was okay to trap people inside his awful dreams and lie about knowing her brother. Andrea didn't understand why he would do it, but whatever his reasons, the Sandman clearly wasn't a friend like he had claimed to be.

Andrea had to find her brother, no matter how many nightmares she had to walk through to do it and no matter what obstacles the Sandman put in her way. Francis was really still out there, tucked away inside the shimmering gates of Reverie, and if she could free herself from the ice and get back to him, she would finally have her chance to bring her brother back and fix what had broken.

Andrea's nostrils flared as she marched with long, bold strides back to the path in the forest that would take her to Reverie's gates, stopping only when her body smacked straight into something firm yet stretchy. It forced her backward, and she landed on her bottom on the snowy ground, as if she had just come up against the side of a giant balloon.

She stood, brushing the snow off her jeans and reaching a hand out toward whatever it was that had sent her back. Sure enough, her fingers pressed into a rubbery barrier of some kind with the images of the forest imprinted upon it. Each branch on each tree looked so detailed and full of dimension, as if it was truly a path instead of a wall. She ran her fingers up, following a slight curve that indicated the shape of a dome rising above her head, where the painted trees gave way to a painted sun and a painted winter sky.

A feeling of relief quickly shifted to frustration that rolled through Andrea like a wave. If this was a dream tent, somehow still a part of the nightmare, or a part of the strangeness that came from staying too long inside one, then a nightmare hadn't collided with the real world and her parents weren't really frozen inside.

But if this was a dream, then she was also trapped; there wasn't an opening or a door anywhere in sight.

Andrea clenched her fists. Even though her entire view of Reverie had flipped upside down in such a short amount of time, she wouldn't quit now. Penny had said there would always be a door. She just had to find it.

And if this was a balloon, then maybe it could pop.

Andrea ran back to the house, bracing herself against its frozen siding. She pushed off, running with all her might toward the barrier that kept her trapped in a world of ice. She gritted her teeth and pumped her arms, the snow kicking up behind each step as she slammed into the dome with the full force of her strength.

The sharp sound of shattering glass entered Andrea's ears and ricocheted inside her head as she stumbled out the backside of *The Frigid Place* tent and landed on the dirt floor of a Reverie lane.

Andrea dusted off her jeans and smiled. She had broken out of the nightmare. Now she had to find her brother.

REMEMBER

Andrea didn't waste time scanning the running, laughing, sticky-fingered children around her for any sign of the boy she had followed into *The Frigid Place*. He probably wouldn't be waiting where she could easily find him. Not as long as the Sandman was working to keep them apart.

She bit her bottom lip, wincing as a pressure grew inside the cracks and holes of her heart and, along with it, a new thought: that maybe the answer of how to move forward lay in the dusty corner she had given up as her price of admission. She had thought it would be so great to let that memory go, and it *had* been great, at least for a little while. She had felt *so much* relief after she woke up in that hammock and the memory was gone. She had lost herself in entire worlds built of dream dust and had felt so free.

She wished she could go back to the moments when the

forgetting had been a comfort, but the relief hadn't been permanent. Too soon, she had felt the invisible hand inside her, skittering around, trying to find what she had lost.

In the end, her heart hadn't really let her forget. She had woken up at home to a confusing mess filled with her mother's tears, and boxes spilled on the lawn, and memories detached from their source. It was clear that trying to forget wasn't the amazing solution she had once thought it would be.

Andrea put a hand to her chest and reminded herself to breathe through the pressure that surged inside her as she realized that maybe, to find out where her brother was, she had to put all the pieces back in place. And doing that would mean entering the memory she had chosen to give away.

If she wanted to find answers about Francis, she would have to un-forget.

✳✳✳

Andrea found her way to a quiet lane of tents containing the memories children gave up to earn their tickets into the dream circus. Each and every one radiated wistfulness and longing, and surrounding them all floated crisp air, like the calm before the first fall of snow, bringing with it the scent of a bonfire burning somewhere far off in the distance.

Now she just had to find her tent. She passed by *Fishing with Grandpa, Our Day in the Woods,* and *The Rainbow Sunset.* It didn't take Andrea long to find herself drawn to one particular tent, much as *Root River* had called to her at the very start. She walked forward, faster and faster, the pull as strong as a magnet until she stopped at the entrance to a tent called *The Night You Left Us.* Every bone inside her body knew this was exactly what she had come down this lane to find.

But as she stood in front of the memory and stared up at the blue and white stripes that contained what she had most wanted to leave behind, knowing what she had to do and actually doing it were two very different things.

The feather and the coin and the vial of sand in Andrea's left pocket emanated a strange sort of heat, almost pushing her forward into the memory. A new voice hummed, soft but insistent inside her. *It has to be him. It has to be him. It has to be him.* The other voice was still there, too. It hissed at her in desperation: *Your fault. Your fault. YOUR FAULT.*

In Andrea's right pocket, the parchment and the charcoal sat, heavy as stone, like they didn't want her to move an inch. Like they expected her to fail. She was about to remember the full extent of her guilt, remember what had happened in the hours between going to bed that final night and waking up the following morning. But maybe she didn't have to. Maybe it wasn't too late. She could still draw a world where nothing bad had ever happened, and all her choices had been the right ones, and the Sandman, good or evil, could attach it to his umbrella and make it come true. It sounded so much easier than walking right into the worst moment of her life and reliving it by choice in the hopes that it might help her find someone who might not even be possible to find.

No.

Running away from everything wasn't an option anymore.

A gust of wind picked up around Andrea, swirling her hair in crazy directions and bringing the bottom of the tents up to billow and wave.

Andrea pulled her hair back with her hands, glancing around, first left, then right. She thought she heard something shuffle behind her. But when she looked back, there was only an empty cotton candy cone rolling down the lane.

Andrea swallowed hard, then stepped inside the memory she had been so eager to give away.

She made the choice to remember.

THE NIGHT YOU LEFT US

Andrea stared at the bunk bed she and Francis used to share. Or, in the world of this dream, still did. The air in the room was heavy with sadness and perfumed with salty tears— and, Andrea quickly realized, a dreamlike version of herself.

The girl on the top bunk was Andrea three years ago, tall for her age, with feathery blonde hair. She shuffled around under her covers, restless. Glow-in-the-dark stars built into constellations on the ceiling above her head offered an eerie green glow to the girl and her deep blue eyes, which were open wide and staring at the ceiling.

She couldn't sleep.

The girl braced herself for the yelling that carried through the door to her and Francis in their room each night. The sounds of anger between her parents that she had gotten used to hearing as she fell asleep.

Now the quiet hung heavy against memory-Andrea's skin, and she tenderly folded her hands together, uncomfortable at the change. Her mom and dad were done with all that now. They wouldn't be able to yell at each other every night if they fell asleep under different roofs. Their whole family was on the edge of a life that would never look the same, and the house was thunderous with silence.

Memory-Andrea sat upright in her bed at the sound of her parents' bedroom door clicking open, then closed. She climbed down the ladder, her bare toes silent on the rungs, then walked forward with careful steps, illuminated by the light from the hallway through their cracked bedroom door.

Andrea followed as the memory version of herself stepped into the hallway, blinking in the brightness, and watched as she tiptoed to the top of the stairs. She looked over the memory's shoulder, down the stairs and toward their front door.

There her father stood, surveying the house, a large suitcase at his side. He fumbled in his pocket, then opened the door and left, the keys clinking in the doorknob as he locked it behind him.

"Dad," memory-Andrea whimpered, too quiet for anyone to hear her. "Please come back. *Please. Come back.*"

Real-Andrea's knees weakened, and she leaned against the railing for support. Watching him leave again now wasn't any easier than it had been to live it the first time.

In her bedroom, the dream version of her brother lay on the bottom bunk and let out a groan in his sleep. "No, no, no!" he yelled, in a voice edged with panic.

Andrea followed as her memory-self ran back to their room and was on the floor beside Francis in two seconds flat. Real-Andrea's entire body ached at the sound of her brother's voice.

"Francis, hey," the memory whispered. "Don't cry. It's okay. I'm here. You're safe."

"No, no, no—please!" He writhed on the mattress, and memory-Andrea reached out, trying to shake him awake.

"Hey, Francis!" she said, louder now. "Wake up, buddy. Wake up!"

Memory-Francis sat bolt upright in bed and opened his eyes, milky white in the moonshine peeking in through the blinds. He blinked once, then twice, his chest heaving, his hand clinging tight to his memory-sister.

Andrea, the one built of flesh and bone, couldn't take it anymore. She lunged forward, her heart surging, reaching out to wrap her arms around this version of her brother. But while the memory bed met her, hard and firm as if it were real, her hand swiped straight through Francis, sending wisps of him sideways like she had brushed through a cloud.

Andrea's shoulders slumped in exhaustion and

disappointment. He looked *so real*. But of course it wasn't really him.

"Buddy, you're okay," memory-Andrea said. "I'm here. It was only a bad dream."

Francis shook his head, his eyes still wide with fear, tears pooling in the bottoms, threatening to plummet down his cheeks.

Memory-Andrea pulled in alongside him on the bed and under the covers. "Want to tell me about it?" she asked.

Francis swallowed.

"It was the same one, the one in the park at night," Francis whispered, flicking his trusting gaze up to meet his sister's. "There was the playground that looked fun. So I walked to it. But I had to cross a river. A big willow tree was there, and it reached out its branches. I thought it would help me cross. I thought it would carry me if I held on to it, but it didn't." He fidgeted with the fabric of the blanket between his fingers. "I reached out to touch its branches, and they pushed me in the river, and I tried to keep going, but the roots of the tree wrapped around me and held me down. I started turning to stone in the river under the water. I started turning into cold, cold stone."

Memory-Andrea bit her bottom lip, while real-Andrea's insides flooded so full of love and longing she worried she might break open from the strain. Here he was, so close, yet untouchable. She had always tried so hard to protect him. Keeping Francis safe had been her job since the moment he was born.

Memory-Andrea's gaze scanned the room before landing on a mason jar sitting on her dresser, filled with beads from a broken bracelet she one day meant to repair. She ran over to it and emptied the beads onto the dresser, where a couple of them rolled to the floor and hid themselves away in the darkness.

"It was just a bad dream, Francis." Memory-Andrea returned to the bed and wrapped her arm around her brother. "And you're awake now. You aren't turning to stone. There's a lot we can't fix right now, but I'm going to fix this for you."

A cloud brushed over the moon outside, and the room grew even dimmer.

Her memory-self held the mason jar out to him. "This is a dream jar," she said. "You can close your eyes and place your bad dream inside it. I'll put the cap on tight and trap the nightmare."

Francis glared at the jar with suspicion.

"It'll work, I promise. First, you have to remember the bad dream and hold it in your hand and press it into the jar. Do you think you can do that for me?"

Francis was quiet for a moment, staring up at the wooden slats supporting the top bunk. Then he spoke with conviction. "Yes," he said. "I can."

Memory-Andrea smiled. "Good. Now close your eyes and press your dream into the jar. I promise, I'll catch it."

Francis sat up and squeezed his eyes closed and clenched his fist, releasing it over the top of the jar. His memory-sister quickly capped it, locking the nightmare inside.

Francis watched as she slid out from the bed, pulled up the blinds, and unlocked the bedroom window, lifting it open and letting a cool breeze rush through.

"Now, I'll let the dream out here. Where it can't bother you anymore."

"Will it really work?" Francis asked, his eyes innocent and eager and desperate for relief.

"You bet it will. No more nightmare. And you'll be able to sleep."

Memory-Andrea stuck her hands far out the open window and opened the jar, lifting her eyes as if watching the nightmare float away before turning back and smiling at her brother.

"That's it?" he asked.

"That's it." Memory-Andrea set the mason jar on her brother's dresser, returned to the bottom bunk, and squeezed Francis's hand. "There's space in your head for a new dream now, and we need to fill it with something good. Think about the most perfect dream. One you'd love to have."

Francis turned to the pictures on his dresser, then lay back down in his bed. His sister rested beside him.

"It would be of our family," Francis said. "All of us. Together."

Memory-Andrea and real-Andrea both winced, then closed their eyes and exhaled. Memory-Andrea spoke, a forced steadiness to her voice. "That sounds like a *perfect* dream. Now close your eyes and imagine the dream from the beginning. The dream where we're all together. And let it send you off to sleep."

Francis closed his eyes while his sister ran her fingers gently through his hair. She sang to her brother, soft and low, the lullaby her mother used to sing to them when they were small enough to be cradled in one arm.

> "Darling I'm here, I'll remain beside you,
> Rest your head, don't be afraid . . ."

The boy's breathing steadied and slowed. Memory-Andrea leaned over her brother, kissed him on the forehead, then returned to the top bunk to fall asleep herself.

And she left the window open.

A gust of wind snaked a path through the bedroom window, nearly knocking real-Andrea sideways as the entire memory accelerated before her eyes. Light and wind and the shadow of tree branches danced wildly on the bedroom walls. The moon arced in the sky over the window and made its way back down to the horizon in a matter of seconds. The night sky lightened, and a hint of dawn turned into full-fledged morning.

Andrea's memory-self sat up in bed, hair wild and cheek crooked-lined with the imprint of wrinkles from her pillow. The sheer white curtains fluttered in the wind, bringing with it the smell of something sweet edged with bitter. Like burnt sugar.

The sound of police sirens floated in through the window.

Her mother was in the yard, screaming Francis's name.

Andrea squinted in the harsh light and padded across the room to look outside.

A police car pulled into the drive. Her father's car pulled in right behind it.

The voice picked up right where it had left off, swimming around in her head like a shark.

Your fault. Your fault. Your fault.

This was it—the reason she'd wanted to forget. She had given up this memory to forget that she was the reason *why* her brother disappeared. Because she had left the window open, allowing something sinister to take him away in the night. Because of her, her brother was gone.

The pang of guilt twisted at her heart, bruising it, cracking it in a hundred different places.

Andrea almost couldn't stand to watch anymore. Wild-eyed, she searched the room, hoping the door would appear so she could stumble back out into Reverie's lanes and attempt to remember to breathe.

But the memory wasn't quite over yet. Something had caught memory-Andrea's eye. Something by the window. The final piece she had lost when she gave the memory to Margaret Grace in order to earn her ticket. Eyes burning and lungs compressed tight, real-Andrea stepped forward so she could see it, too.

There, on the windowsill, glittering under the sun, was a small vial of shimmering sand.

Memory-Andrea snatched the vial off the windowsill just as real-Andrea reached into her own pocket. Memory-Andrea stared at the vial in her open palm just as real-Andrea pulled out the vial of remaining sand and held it in *her* open palm, too. The memory-girl clutched it tightly before walking out of the room to look for the brother she would never find.

This was how she had gotten the vial of sand. Someone had wanted her to find it.

The door to the hallway flickered, a wave of silver light passing through it. The exit to the memory had appeared.

There. Something shuffled behind her again just as it had before she first entered the tent. Something tucked away in the corner.

The hair on the back of Andrea's neck stood on end.

It could be anything. It could be a dream bug, or a random kid, or Penny.

Andrea hoped it was something—or someone—else entirely, and she couldn't stop the electric hope that seized her and now pulsed through her veins. The hope that maybe if Andrea knew Francis was in Reverie, maybe he knew she was in Reverie, too. And if he had followed her into her tent, then some part of him must want them to be together. Even if someone else wanted to keep them apart.

She had to let him know it was okay. She had to, as she had on so many sleepless nights, make him feel safe.

Andrea froze in place, the vial of sand clutched in her hand, and cleared her dry throat. Then, voice wavering, she picked up where the lullaby had left off in the dream.

> **"Darling I'm here, I'll remain beside you.**
> **Rest your head, don't be afraid.**
> **You'll find me,**

Shine light to the shadows.

And carry you into the break of day."

Dust particles floated lazily past the window, but all else in the room stood still. Andrea's heart sank. Maybe she had imagined the noise. Maybe she had, once again, filled herself with useless hope. The kind of hope she had felt whenever the phone rang with a tip from someone claiming to have seen her brother. Claims that all turned out to be hoaxes. Twisted lies whispered by twisted people.

Lies like the promise of Reverie. The promise of blissful escape.

A voice spoke softly behind her. "Please, don't be mad," it said.

Andrea's heart seized.

FOUND

The voice Andrea thought she might never hear again entered her ears and wove through her body, filling a bit of the hole inside her weak and tired heart.

"How could I be mad?" she said, her voice shaking as she turned to face her brother. "I've been looking for you for such a long time."

Francis ran toward his sister, warm arms wrapping themselves around Andrea's waist. She embraced her brother, falling to her knees. Francis folded himself into her, like he had so many times before.

He was real. He was *here*.

Tension bled from Andrea's limbs, relief leaving her weak, wrung out like her mother's dishrag hanging over the sink. She held her brother while he cried, clinging to him, breathing in the sweet scent of his hair and hugging her arms around his small frame. Too small, she realized.

Francis's tears slowed, and he pulled back from their embrace. His face tilted to the floor. "I didn't mean to run away . . . I thought you'd be mad at me. The Sandman warned me you would be mad and said I shouldn't let you find me. Even though I wanted to give you a big hug, I was scared you'd yell or tell Mom and Dad. But I just couldn't keep doing what the Sandman said. I missed you so much." He lifted his sad, guilty eyes to his sister. Eyes with the same deep purple circles under them as she had seen on all of the other Reverie children.

Anger grew once more inside Andrea at the Sandman, who pretended to be friendly but who lied. Who had kept her brother away from home for such a long time. "The last thing I could ever be is mad at you, Francis. And I'm sure Mom and Dad will feel exactly the same."

He sniffed and wiped his nose on his pajama sleeve. "You look different," he said. "How did you get so tall?"

Andrea bit her lip. Here he was, the same size and in the same pajamas as the night he disappeared. Her brother hadn't aged. He was still the six-year-old boy she'd lost. Time hadn't touched him. "How long do you think you've been here, buddy?" she asked, not sure how to find a way to tell him the truth and also not sure why her brother hadn't gotten older.

Francis sat on the floor, drumming his fingers on his knees, while Andrea sat beside him, their hands intertwined. "That's a hard question. I had the bad dream at home, and then you stuck it in the jar and I thought of the nice dream and fell back asleep. But I woke up a little while later. And I was so, so hungry." Francis rubbed a hand over his stomach. "And some *amazing* smells were coming through the window. It smelled like the fair. I went to the window, and outside it the street was gone and there was a forest and a friendly girl and a big circus behind a tall gate. It was like I could step right outside our window, Drea, and into a new *world*. The girl said they had found my nightmare and wanted to keep it somewhere it would be safe. They wanted to trade my nightmare in and give me a wish, my perfect dream. The one you told me I should try to have, of our family, all together. And the girl also said if I came with her I could come in and eat whatever I want." His face pinched up, like it always did when he confessed to doing something he wasn't supposed to do, like watching TV when he shouldn't, or coloring on the walls. "So I said yes, and I met the Sandman, and he turned my nightmare into a tent I never had to go in again."

"I know," Andrea said, touching a hand to his cheek. "I was in that dream. That's how I knew to look for you."

"I watched you go in. I don't like that other kids go in my

nightmare. I wait there sometimes. I try to warn them away."
Francis picked at a piece of loose carpet, squinting hard at
the strands. "He drew me my wish and tucked it inside his
umbrella and made it real. It was our home, but without anything sad. I wanted to remember being happy, before Mom
and Dad started to fight."

Andrea wrapped her arm around Francis's shoulder.
Her eyes burned as she remembered all the emptiness over
the past three years since they lost him. The Christmases,
Thanksgivings, all with an extra empty seat at the table. And
the normal days in between, too. No one next to her on the
floor doing homework. No one to ride her bike with through
the woods. To watch cartoons with on Saturday morning.

Out of instinct, Andrea's hand reached into her pocket for
comfort as she wrapped her fingers around the vial of shimmering sand.

"Francis," she asked. "Did you leave anything behind
for me in the window . . . before you went through Reverie's
gates? Maybe something to help me find you, or follow you,
even?"

Francis tipped his head. "I don't think so," he said. "I don't
think I looked back."

"Oh. That's okay," Andrea said. "I just thought I'd ask."

If Francis hadn't been the one to leave the sand on the

window, then Andrea was out of answers as to how it got there. She couldn't imagine it had just appeared by chance right after Francis had disappeared inside Reverie. But the most important thing was that her brother was here with her now. *Found.*

"It's been a long night," Francis said, switching his fidgeting fingers to the hem of his pajama shirt. "I didn't know nights could be this long."

Andrea's shoulders curled forward, her chest caving in. She swallowed hard. Francis thought he had been here for one night, like their ticket said.

"Buddy," she said, taking a wide breath in preparation. "I'm not sure how to tell you this, but you've been here longer than one night."

Francis looked at her, his eyebrows squished together and a perfect frown on his innocent face. "How long have I been here?"

Andrea stared at the hem of her jeans, then forced her gaze up to meet his. "You noticed I got taller."

"Yeah. So?"

"Well," she said. "I'm not sure how any of this works yet. But I promise I'm going to figure it out so I can bring you home. One thing I do know is I'm twelve and you're supposed to be nine, but you still look like you're six. You've been here for three years. We've been looking for you for three long, long years."

Francis's face washed to white, further accenting the deep, sleepless purple circles.

Andrea drew her brother in closer as the burning in her eyes grew almost too much to bear. But she had to stay strong for him, at least until she got them both safely home.

"I'm so sorry, Francis. I never should have left the window open. I'm so, *so* sorry."

Francis, still very pale, pulled back from Andrea with a slight shake of his head. "This isn't your fault. You were just trying to help me."

"But if I hadn't done all that stupid stuff with your dream . . ."

"No. It isn't your fault," he said again, his voice firm.

Andrea watched her brother's face. It was the same face he made when he was about to put in the last piece of a tricky puzzle. Like he was about to win.

"It's my fault," he said.

"How is this possibly your fault?" Andrea asked, cupping his face in her hands. "There's no way you're the one to blame. If you believe anything, you've got to believe that."

Francis shook her off. "I *chose* to go. The girl tricked me into coming, but I chose to believe her. I wanted something nice to happen. I was so mad in real life. And living in a world where our family wasn't broken sounded so nice. But I promise, I didn't know what they meant, I didn't know I'd be gone so long." Tears slipped down his cheeks. "I thought it was one night. I thought it was a dream."

Nothing about what her brother said sat well inside her. Maybe neither of them was truly to blame, at least as much as she had once thought. Maybe the one to blame was the person who invited kids here in the first place and didn't tell them the whole story.

"We have to get out of this house," Andrea said as another couple of children entered the tent and the dream room darkened back into night. "It's time to go home. And I promise you, we're going home together."

"Okay," Francis said, but he didn't make a move. Instead, he stared longingly at the dresser filled with pictures of a family that had not yet broken. The same pictures Andrea had spilled out of the box in their front yard.

"Are Mom and Dad still—" He cut off the words, but Andrea knew what he was asking. He wanted to know if their parents were still apart. She pulled her little brother in close, rubbing her hand on the top of his soft head and giving it a gentle kiss.

It was all the answer he needed to hear. "Oh," he said, disappointed. "I thought I was dreaming, so I thought I was asleep the whole time. But I'm also really, really tired."

"You look tired," Andrea said as a knot formed in her belly. Francis hadn't slept in three years. Maybe the deep circles weren't even from sleep deprivation but from living so long in a place between sleeping and awake. Whatever the case, Francis would get rest soon, because Andrea was going home and she was taking him with her.

***

"Come on," Andrea said, this time leading her brother to the door that would take them back to the Reverie grounds.

Francis sighed, turning back once more to the pictures on his dresser before following her out of the tent.

Andrea put her arm around Francis's shoulder. They walked past the Dream Clock and down the fairway to Reverie's gates, which were closed and firmly locked.

"Hey!" Andrea wrapped her fingers around the bars and peered through them for any sign of Margaret Grace. If she could open the gates to let kids in, Andrea had to imagine she could open them to let kids out. But Margaret Grace didn't come when Andrea called.

Andrea looked up at the sky. The stars were still out, the moon still hung directly above their heads, lower and larger than normal, though it was probably just another one of Reverie's tricks.

An eerie silence pervaded beyond the iron gate, a marked contrast to the buzz of Reverie behind them.

"I see you've been reunited! How lovely!"

Andrea jumped back.

The Sandman stood beside her, having appeared out of nowhere, standing way too close and smiling down at her with shiny white teeth. He took in a deep, satisfied breath through his nose. "My dear Margaret and I used to have such fun running amok in and out of Reverie's tents." He paused, his voice changing, becoming deep and assertive. "Andrea, have you decided what wondrous wish you would like me to build for you? I trust you still have the paper."

This was it. Her time had come. She clasped on to Francis's hand and held it tight. "You told me you didn't know my brother."

"Ah, that." The Sandman shifted his weight. "A misunderstanding, I assure you. I was *truly* hoping you'd find each other after all. I want nothing more than for my Dreamers to find their wishes fulfilled inside Reverie's walls."

Andrea eyed the Sandman with suspicion. She didn't buy it. Not one cent. But it wasn't the time to argue over the man's lies. It was time to go home.

"Thank you," Andrea said, "for all you've done to make Reverie, but no thank you all the same. I won't be needing a wish. My parents and I have been missing my brother for three years. He didn't mean to stay in Reverie this long. I want to bring him back. *He* wants to come back. I'd like to take him home." Andrea nodded to Francis, who nodded to the Sandman.

"It's been . . . fun," Francis added awkwardly, "but I didn't know how long I was gone."

"Our parents are worried," Andrea said, conveying more confidence with her voice than she felt. She stared hard at the imposing man, refusing to let her fear peek through. She had to hope some part of him would understand.

Francis squeezed Andrea's hand tightly. They waited for the Sandman to open the gates, to tell them it was quite all right, that he'd made a mistake. That the boy and his sister would be allowed to go home.

Instead, the façade of kindness on the Sandman's face melted away and was replaced by something with harder edges. The face a parent makes when there is no room to negotiate around their choice. He clicked his shining black heels together, locking himself in place.

"Oh dear," he said, folding both hands over the hook of the umbrella, more to himself than to the two of them. "This was bound to happen at some point, wasn't it?"

"What?" Andrea and Francis said at the exact same moment as dread crept up Andrea's stomach and wrapped its ropelike tendrils around her heart. The scent in the fairway turned metallic and sour, as if she could actually smell the iron fence with the poking starbursts at the top, keeping them inside.

"Your desire to go home together, obviously," he said, sharper now, and louder. Sterner. He punctuated the horror of the moment by tipping his face, shrouding most of it in inky shadows as his words echoed like an unwelcome song through the nearly empty space. "Dear children, I'm sorry, but it isn't possible for you to leave."

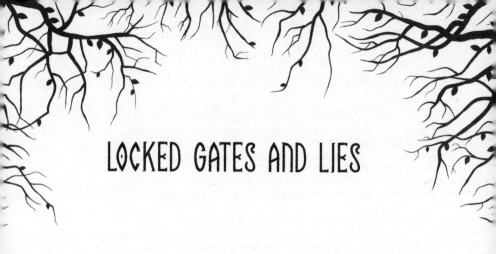

LOCKED GATES AND LIES

Andrea's legs threatened to buckle beneath her. She reached out for something to hold on to, grabbing the corner of one of the nearby shops at the end of the fairway, painted in sea-glass green and offering things like scales from mermaids' tails and tendrils from deep-sea witches. Salty air wafted from the shop's open windows, enough for her to find her footing and her focus.

"But I've already left," Andrea said, her voice biting. "I went home. I woke up on my floor and tried to stop my parents from giving away Francis's things."

"Did you truly go home?" the Sandman asked softly, as if reeling in a fish caught on a hook, letting her wriggle at every drawn-out word. "Did you wake up in your real room, Andrea? Did you ever leave Reverie through the gates?"

Andrea didn't answer. Didn't understand what he was

getting at, what the Sandman was trying to say. She thought back to the morning when she had woken up on the floor. She had left Reverie.

But not through the gates.

She just . . . woke up, believing Reverie had all been a dream. She hadn't given it any thought at the time, but when she came to back inside Reverie she'd woken up on the ground in the exact same spot where everything had melted around her.

Andrea grimaced as dread curled like smoke all around her and the chilling reality settled itself deep inside her bones: She had entered Reverie last night . . . and she had *never* left.

"I don't understand," Andrea pleaded, the heat behind her eyes building. "Why did it look like I woke up in my room?"

"That much is simple," the Sandman explained, his voice cold and detached. "You broke a Reverie rule. You tried to remember the memory you gave up to earn your ticket without going through the tent. And when you do that, things . . . malfunction. The lines between dream and reality tend to blur. It can all be quite confusing. Which is why we warn you at the start not to do it. If you break the rules, the dreams have a way of sticking," he said, his mouth bending down into a scowl. He lifted his shoe to find a tacky substance pulling slowly upward from the earth. "Like gum under your shoe." He shook off the gum, sneaking a glance back at the Reverie crowds.

Andrea hadn't pinched herself when she woke up that morning—hadn't thought she needed to because she had woken up *in her room*. She understood now that if she had, she would have felt nothing, because it was all part of a terrible, awful dream.

Everything else Andrea had experienced since she arrived shifted then in her mind, taking on sharp edges and crystal-clear features. She hadn't just stayed too long inside a nightmare. She was still living it. Reverie morphed itself into whatever appearance it wanted, a circus, her home, her room. It had no limits. And it was very, and horribly, real.

She had assumed that the starbursts on the top of the fence were meant to keep kids from getting in for free. But they were really meant to keep kids trapped inside the Sandman's prison. A prison that lulled you into thinking it was only make-believe.

The heat behind her eyes grew, and with it, the threat of tears to put out the flame.

"Don't cry, child."

"I never cry!" Andrea flinched as the Sandman tried to pat her on the head, ducking out of the way.

The Sandman looked so different from the friendly images on the Dream Clock and the balloons, and the memorabilia lining the windows of so many shops. Andrea knew now that he didn't only *look* different from the pictures of the old, gentle man plastered all over this place. She knew now that his heart was hard and dark and cold. And cruel.

The Sandman pulled his hands back, holding them up in surrender. "I never meant for you to fear me, dear one. I'm only trying to help you understand that this is for the best."

The Sandman snapped his fingers, and Margaret Grace, the littlest girl from his dream, walked out from behind a corner and joined hands with her ringmaster brother, smiling at Andrea and Francis. He snapped them again, and the version of Margaret Grace from Reverie's gates came out and stood next to the first. One final snap, and the Margaret Grace in the ball gown from the center of the Sandman's private dream joined them, too.

"Margaret and I used to escape to Reverie often, didn't we? This little world of my creation," the Sandman said, looking dotingly down at the youngest version of his sister. "We'd run, zigging and zagging in and out of shops and tents, laughing and screaming and playing each night together before returning home."

The youngest Margaret Grace grinned up at her brother. Then her face went vacant, wiped of expression. She turned around, facing her back to them all, head hung low.

"We grew, and still Reverie was our greatest comfort.

Neither Margaret nor I had an easy time at home. We survived on our dreams. We inhaled them, breathed them in, ate them for dinner when there was no food in the cupboards." The Margaret from the gates hung her head and turned around like the first.

"But my Margaret grew weary of dreaming." He circled around the oldest version of his sister, who stared straight ahead, a quiet defiance on her face. "She offered to join me in Reverie one final time. She built the tent and sang the most beautiful song in front of an adoring crowd. And oh, how they cheered for her!" The Sandman paused, tipping his head and staring into his sister's face. "After that night, I asked her to return to Reverie with me. To see if we could stay here forever, safe and happy and *together*. I *begged* her to see if we could stay. Why remain in a world that turned its back on us when we could have all *this*? But she insisted she was through."

The Sandman turned back to Andrea and Francis. "A week later, my sister . . . my"—his voice cracked, and his eyes, dark as tunnels, brimmed with tears—"my precious sister contracted cholera and *died*." The final Margaret Grace hung her head, too, and turned her back to them all.

Andrea fought against the Sandman's story with everything she had inside her, but it set itself up like a mirror to her own suffering and pain. She closed her eyes a moment, determined to avoid seeing herself reflected in this horrible man and his desperate choices.

"She isn't real," Andrea insisted, turning her gaze to the strange set of dream sisters. "None of them are real."

"Would you rather go back? Truly?" The Sandman lifted his chin. "To a world where there is no magic? Where people we love die, and parents split up, and brothers disappear?" He crept closer to them. "Your brother wanted to escape a shattered world. A world where his family was breaking and there was nothing he could do to stop it. And now he gets to *stay*."

"This wasn't what he meant," Andrea said, gripping tight to her brother's hand where he hid behind her. "He didn't mean to never come home."

"And you!" The Sandman leaned toward her, hovering over her head, blocking out the light of the round, fat moon with his hat.

"You so badly wanted to escape a world where you lost your brother, where people pitied the child who wasn't meant to be alone. Where even your parents had given up hoping they'd find him. I've done nothing but grant your wish. It took some extra magic . . ." He peered over the top of Andrea's head at a cowering Francis, as if that somehow proved his point. "But I brought you to a world where your brother could be found."

Where her brother *could be found.*

The Sandman's choice of words slammed into her heart like a tidal wave on a stormy sea. If he knew her heart's biggest, truest wish was to find her little brother . . . was the boy with her now really Francis? The real, living, breathing brother she had lost?

Or—her heart surged in pain as if someone had shocked it—was he also somehow part of the nightmare she was trapped in, like the Sandman's dream versions of Margaret Grace? A brother built for her out of the strongest of Reverie's magic, a dream who was warm to the touch but who would burn away like the crawling mist at dawn.

Andrea pulled Francis around to her front and clutched him tightly, smelling his still-sweet hair and holding his shaking frame as he clung to her, trusting her to make this right.

She grasped at the thin thread of hope that maybe the Sandman didn't mean what he had implied. Andrea had already lost Francis once, and it nearly broke her. She would dissolve into slivers of flesh and blood and shattered heart if she lost her brother a second time.

One thing was for certain: Andrea wasn't going to pull Francis into the seed of doubt the Sandman had placed inside her head.

"It may not be the answer you hoped for, but it is for the

best if you stay," the Sandman continued. "After all, what kind of person would I be if I offered children safety, and joy, and escape, then sent them back out into a world that would only bring them pain and suffering in the end?" A single tear fell in a jagged line down the Sandman's face. "Yes. Indeed. It is certainly better that you should have to stay."

The Sandman offered his arm as if he meant to tuck them into the fold. "Now come, children," he said as Andrea and Francis recoiled. "There are many, many wonders you have yet to see. There's no point in dwelling on useless things when one is in a land of dreams."

"I'll keep them company!"

Andrea and Francis jumped.

Penny sprung out from the doorway of the empty shop. "I have no interest in going home, sir. And, gee, I know almost everything about this place." She stuck her hands on her hips and passed a devious, knowing smile to the Sandman. The Sandman smiled back, as if pleased at last to find another who understood him.

It was disgusting. All of it. That Penny would want to be part of the Sandman's twisted game, part of keeping children here against their will. But now at least it all made sense. Penny's hesitation to bother the Sandman, and how impor-tant it was to her that he liked her. Andrea felt ridiculous now for ever having trusted her. Penny had been on the Sandman's side the whole time.

Andrea stared hard at the smug expression on Penny's face, trying to reconcile the girl standing before her now with the girl she had met on the fairway. She had seemed so sincere, maybe even overeager at times to have someone she could call a friend. And after Andrea survived *Root River* and started looking for Francis, Penny had insisted that all the children were only there for one night.

Andrea grasped at the possibility that maybe the Sandman was lying to Penny, too. That maybe, like the other Reverie children, Penny didn't know the whole story.

The only reason Andrea knew how much time had passed was because she had lived three entire years in the real world without a brother. Without that, she would have had no reason to doubt that time simply "worked differently" in dreams. She would have run through the lanes like all the other Reverie children, thinking she had been granted one magically long night.

Maybe *that* was the reason the Sandman had tried so hard to keep her away from Francis. Francis was proof that Reverie children had been there a long, long time.

If he really was her brother.

Andrea shook the doubts off her shoulders, refusing to

let them pull her down, sink her into despair. She would deal with what the Sandman said later. Right now she had a scared little boy beside her who might just be the one she had lost, and she wasn't about to leave him behind.

And then there was Penny.

Andrea couldn't be the only person in Reverie who had been fed the Sandman's lies.

"Do you even know how long *you've* been here?" Andrea snapped at Penny.

"What does it matter?" the Sandman snapped back.

Penny gave a slight flinch, maybe, then continued to smirk, hip popped and chin held high, like she owned the place. If Andrea had caught Penny off guard, Penny sure hid it well.

"We have to get out of here," Andrea whispered to Francis. "Listen carefully and do exactly as I say. We're going to back up slowly. On the count of three, we run."

Francis gave a slight nod, without taking his eyes off the Sandman.

"One," they took a step backward.

"Children," the Sandman said. "Where on earth are you going? There's no need to run. You're safe here. You'll be safe forever."

"Two." They took another step.

"Oh," the Sandman said, shaking his head. "This is quite unnecessary, I assure you."

"*Friends*," Penny pleaded with them. "Let me show you around. Please! I promise it'll all be fine!"

"Three!" Andrea and Francis spun away from the Sandman and, hand in hand, ran as fast as they could down the fairway.

TWISTING LANES

"We'll find the end of a lane and climb over the fence," Andrea yelled to Francis as they ran. She didn't care if she got poked with the stars at the top. She could handle a little bit of pain, protect Francis with her own body if she had to, if that's what it took to get out of this nightmare for good.

"Got it!" he shouted back, his sweet little voice determined.

Andrea slowed a little so Francis wouldn't fall behind with his much shorter legs. He scanned the lanes, his eyes wide-open and alert. Andrea hoped the adrenaline would last long enough for them to find a way to get free.

They turned down the lane that contained Francis's nightmare and so many others, running straight past it while half expecting to see the Sandman jump out from behind every shadow. They wove around groups of tired-eyed children, squealing and cackling, feverish from Reverie's thrills. Children who had been there for decades, or even *centuries*, maybe. The fence poked out through the gaps in the tents at certain angles and beyond where the lanes curved. Andrea led Francis, cheeks flushed and arms pumping, toward one of the spaces, pushing herself between the walls of thick canvas.

"Come on," Andrea said, turning and reaching a hand back to pull her brother through a particularly tight opening as the shadow of a top hat passed along the dream tent to their right. The fence stood just a few feet away. "We're almost there."

When she turned forward, the space between the tents had changed. Where only moments before it had been an access point to the fence, it now opened up to another long Reverie lane, the fence only visible through the gaps in another set of tents a long distance away.

Undeterred, Andrea and Francis ran down the sloping lane and pulled forward once more between the tents. This time Andrea reached out her hand to clasp the iron bars. She didn't turn away as they drew near.

But in a single blink the fence was suddenly gone, replaced by another long stretch of tents, the fence once again a long distance beyond it.

"It isn't possible for you to leave . . ." The Sandman's words snaked past them in an unwelcome wind. Heat singed

Andrea's stomach, but this wouldn't defeat her, no matter what twisted game the Sandman had decided to play. They wouldn't stop. They were going to find a way to escape.

Andrea and Francis ran and ran and ran some more. The fence melted into stripes of blue and white before her eyes as she reached out to touch it, or the lanes bent backward around themselves so they couldn't get near the edge. Silhouettes of umbrellas danced along the sides of the striped tents, teasing them. It was as if the Sandman was rearranging the dreams as they went, letting them know he kept up with their every move. Andrea glanced up at the Dream Clock in the center as they pursued the edge of a circus that had turned into a twisting, senseless maze. They ran until Andrea's chest burned with every breath and her legs ran out of strength. They made their way to the other side of the Dream Clock entirely, without ever crossing past it and without ever reaching the end of a lane.

"I have to stop," Francis huffed. His footsteps slowed behind her and he bent over, his chest heaving in and out.

Andrea put a hand on Francis's back. "Breathe, buddy," she said. "It's okay, just breathe." She kicked the dirt and looked around the lane, at all the children going merrily along their way as if everything was fine while the Sandman had tricked her and Francis into running out their strength, taking pleasure in their futile attempt to get free.

Still, Andrea had seen Reverie's gate and the fence around it before she even came inside. It didn't go on forever and ever. It was contained within a field in the woods behind her house.

Though it *had* seemed so much bigger than the field even the first time she saw it, and Margaret Grace had said it could be in more than one place at once so the kids who needed Reverie could find it.

There had to be a way out, even if it was back the way they'd come. Back to the one place she had ever touched Reverie's edge.

"We're going to have to go back to the gate, Francis," Andrea said, still breathing heavily.

Francis's face turned ashen. "But he's watching us. What if he's there? Or his dream sister? What if they're guarding it?"

He *had* been watching them, but they had no other chance of escaping if they could never even reach the fence. Andrea set her jaw as she scanned a path to the fairway. "Right now we're stuck if we stay in the middle. We have to at least try."

"Okay . . . okay," Francis said, bringing himself back to standing. "I can get to the gate. But it's just so high . . . and spiky."

Francis was right.

Maybe the way out of this place wasn't over the fence at all.

Maybe it was *under*.

"Francis . . . I think we should make a quick stop on our way over. We need to find a shovel."

A flash of understanding sparked in Francis's eyes. The two siblings ran off with a single mission: enter the pirate dream and emerge with a shovel from the treasure hunt.

Once they had succeeded, they took off once more, this time straight past the Dream Clock and toward the crowded fairway, which buzzed, as ever, with moving children.

"Stay with me, Francis!" Andrea shouted behind her. She bumped shoulders with a kid in burlap pants rushing in the direction of the Dream Clock tower, shouting: "The show's starting in the square! C'mon!"

A girl in crimson ballet shoes stood on pointe and juggled sparkling sticks above her black-and-white-painted face. A silver mime boy watched them, from his perch on top of a post, the only stillness in a sea of movement. Hordes of children gathered on the fairway, their faces blurring together as Andrea and Francis pushed upstream toward Reverie's gate.

The crowd heading to the square built itself tighter and tighter around them, and Andrea's muscles strained against the current, pushing against the frenzied, bumping bodies toward their goal. Above waves of bobbing heads, the gate stood as far away as ever even after they had spent themselves again with effort. Andrea couldn't tell if this was another trick, if the Sandman had used his magic once more to interfere, or if it was all in her head and the exhaustion from being stuck here was once again messing up her ability to tell the difference between what was fake and what was real.

Andrea's breath hitched as she caught a glimpse of herself in the shop filled with enchanted mirrors. Her own eyes now bore a slight purple hue beneath them. Not as deep as some of the other children, but enough to let Andrea know she had definitely stayed in Reverie longer than one night.

"Andrea!" Francis called to her, his voice pleading. Andrea turned only to see her little brother being sucked backward into the crowd headed for the show. His hand reached for her, but the pack of children closed in quickly around him, carrying him away.

"Francis!" This was *not* going to end with her losing her brother again. Not when they were this close to going home.

The pleasant delirium and the buzz of Reverie's enchantment and the terror woven into all its nightmares whirled around Andrea, slow at first, then faster and faster like a carousel gone wild. Andrea saw the faces of her parents, frozen in their own home, her father's eyes, wet and begging to be freed. The laughing boy outside the jester's tent. Penny's lonely face, staring after Andrea as she left her behind. Shimmering sand and lost dreams and sleep as black as death. Lost children and lost years and sweet candy tainted bitter. And a circus that hovered somewhere outside time but showed up at the exact moment a child was vulnerable enough to venture inside it. A hungry spider in a plum top hat, wrapping writhing victims inside its web.

And Francis.

The little boy she had comforted in his bed before he disappeared. His fear when she found him, tucked away, hidden in a dream. His sad, trusting eyes when she promised to bring him home. Her hope that he was real.

Andrea lunged into the sea of people.

"Francis!" She toppled children over, shoving them out of her way, then stumbling over a set of legs, falling forward, her body slamming into the hard dirt. From there, she caught sight of Francis's striped pajamas behind a flurry of stomping feet, barely close enough to touch.

"Francis!" Andrea curled her fingers around the fabric and pulled his leg toward her. Her brother's desperate, fear-filled face turned to hers in slow motion compared to the wild movement that had almost pulled them apart. Andrea knelt in the middle of the swarms of children and pulled her brother in tight, taking the brunt of the bumping bodies and stomping feet on her own bones.

All grew quiet as the chaos of Reverie faded like the calm

in the middle of a storm. In that moment there was no Reverie. No Sandman, no lost children, no lost years. There was only Andrea and Francis. A sister who held her long-lost brother tightly inside her arms. His sweet-smelling hair and the body that folded easily into hers.

"Come on," she said, squeezing his hand. "I've got you. Let's go."

A shovel in one hand and Francis's hand in the other, Andrea led her brother past the edge of the crowd, to where the fairway opened up and Reverie's gates stood, tall and black as night.

The place where this nightmare would end.

WHAT YEAR DID YOU COME HERE?

Andrea stuck the shovel into the packed dirt, pressed it down with the heel of her shoe, then tossed the earth aside. Once. Then again. None of the Margaret Graces were around. Maybe they had returned to their respective rooms in the Sandman's private dream. And if the Sandman was watching, he hadn't done anything to stop them so far. Maybe he had gotten bored with the two of them and was busy with dream versions of his sister, pretending he lived in a world where she wasn't really gone. Whatever the reason, Andrea was going to take advantage and make progress under the fence.

A crack zipped through the air, shaking the ground beneath them. Andrea and Francis turned to find the entrails of a golden firework descending, slow and graceful through the sky. Then another, with sparks of blue and white like Reverie's tents. And more still, the colors of the sun and the moon and the clouds. Silver like the Sandman's dream dust. They filled the black sky and danced in front of the moon.

If things had been different, Andrea would have watched the entire show. Would have jumped at another opportunity to embrace Reverie's magical distraction, happy to have fallen under its spell. Even with her determination, she couldn't help but sneak a few peeks at the sky. Everything about this place was designed to draw you in deeper, if you didn't know any better.

At least the fairway had nearly emptied of children for the time being, which would give her less of a chance of being noticed while she dug their way free.

Andrea cast a quick glance at her brother, the words the Sandman had chosen to use still rolling around in the rough waters of her mind. He created a world where Francis *could be found*. The cracked and missing pieces of her heart hurt at how badly she wanted this boy to be the real Francis. How badly she wanted the chance to bring him home. Maybe even to reunite her family, to fix all the broken things. If nothing was shattered anymore, then she could fill in all the missing pieces of herself. She wouldn't have to pull away from the world around her for fear of breaking.

Andrea dug into the dirt again, and again, and again. Within a few minutes, her hands grew hot from the friction, and at least a couple of blisters had begun to form, a ridge of small, white mounds of skin across her heated palms.

Andrea froze mid-scoop of earth as a darkness fell over her shovel. A darkness with a head and two pigtails sticking out at the sides. Francis stumbled backward, nearly knocking Andrea over. She dropped the shovel and caught her brother before he fell. Both of them pivoted, bracing themselves for betrayal.

"What year did you come here?" Penny asked, breathing through her nose, her arms hanging straight down, her fists clenched tight.

"Stay away from us." Andrea pulled Francis behind her and looked past Penny for any sign of the Sandman. There was only the fairway, the shops, the shadows of the children huddled in the square.

"Please." Penny held up her hand. Her pink cheeks were stained with the paths of many tears, and bloodshot lines ran through the whites of her tired eyes. "I won't tell the Sandman what you're doing. I just need to know what year it was when you came. *Please.*"

Andrea eyed Penny, tried to figure out what she was all about. Either she was on the Sandman's side and was doing some award-winning acting right now, or Andrea had been right—Penny was a girl who had just figured out she'd been here way longer than one night and was trying to put the pieces of her own puzzle together.

"Andrea," Francis peeked out from behind her. "She looks really sad."

Andrea couldn't disagree. But still, she wasn't sure if this girl could be trusted. "How do we know this isn't a trick?" she whispered to Penny.

"Because thanks to you I know the Sandman is a liar. And I think he's been lying to everyone for . . . a really long time. That's why I wanted you to take me with you when you tried to get away. I saw you and Francis together and followed you to the gate. I hid in the shop. I believe you've found your brother, and I heard *everything* about how long he's been gone." Penny nodded to Francis. Her voice softened. "I need to know how long I've been gone, too."

Andrea looked between Francis and Penny. Francis nodded, breaking down the last bit of Andrea's hesitation. If Penny turned out to be a snitch, they would have to get smarter and try harder to escape. But if she really was a lost girl, Andrea couldn't withhold the answer to her question. Even when she suspected that Penny had also been gone much longer than she thought.

"2020. I came here in October 2020," Andrea said. "Francis disappeared in the same month, on the twenty-first, in 2017."

Penny's pink cheeks drained of color. Her fists fell limp at her sides.

Francis took a step toward her, speaking with the same genuine innocence in his voice as he always had when asking Andrea how her day had been, or if she wanted to play a game with him, or about what made the clouds.

"When did you get here, Penny?" he asked.

Penny shook her head in short, quick movements, unable to speak.

"It's okay, Penny. We're friends," Francis said. "You can tell us. You're safe."

Penny's gaze met Andrea's, then fell to Francis, her eyes brimming with regret and bordered by tense, fresh fear.

Andrea widened her stance, bracing herself for Penny's answer. "He's right, Penny," she said. "You can tell us."

Penny swallowed and stared up at the iron gate that held them all locked inside and spoke with a voice as empty and as hollow as the hole they were attempting to dig.

"I entered Reverie in 1956."

Andrea's soul hurt. She took a tentative step toward the

girl, clearly seeing now the high-waisted dress, the pigtails, the white socks folded over shiny black saddle shoes. "Oh, Penny," she murmured. "That was over sixty years ago."

Andrea and Francis ran to their friend and wrapped her in a hug that felt so needed but could never possibly be enough.

THE DIG

They pulled away from Penny as she tipped her head to the shovel and the growing mound of dirt beside it.

"Do you think he's just going to let you dig a hole under the gate?" Penny swiped the drying streams of tears on her cheeks with the back of her hand.

"He hasn't stopped us yet, and we've been at it for a while," Andrea said, wincing at the pain in her palms and at the words she had chosen. They had figured out time in Reverie was twisted, messed up, folded over on itself. She didn't want to think about how long in earth time they had been digging already or how long she herself had been gone.

Andrea shivered and slammed the shovel back into the dirt.

"I've never seen anyone leave," Penny said. "Then again, I've never seen anyone care enough to try."

"Same," said Francis.

Penny glanced back at the Dream Clock. "And if this works . . . if I leave with you and end up in your year . . ." Her voice trailed off as a wave of fresh tears filled the bottoms of her eyes. She pulled her lips to the side. "What if I'm old? What if I stayed here so long I missed my own life?"

Andrea reached out and took hold of Penny's hand.

"I sometimes feel older than I look. *So* much older." Penny exhaled, a rueful expression on her face as she counted the years on her fingers. "In the real world, if I had a normal life, I'd probably be a grandma. I'd have grandkids, and I'd give them lemonade and shortbread cookies, and I'd make sure they felt like they were the most special kids in the whole wide world like my grandma always does . . . or *did*, for me." She tried to blink back the tears, but they fell anyway.

Andrea gave Penny's hand a tight squeeze and continued to dig.

Francis kept watch for any sign of the Sandman while Andrea and Penny took turns. One shovelful at a time, they carved a hole under the iron gate. Andrea used some of the time to fill Penny in on how she found her brother and what the memory she had given up had contained. She even showed Penny the vial of sand she had kept in her pocket from the night Francis disappeared. The rest of the time they tried to sort out everything that had transpired since the Sandman said they couldn't go home.

Even if there were kids that wanted to stay, nothing about Reverie was right. Even if a kid wanted to escape a world where they felt like they didn't fit, it wasn't fair to take them away forever, trapping them in a make-believe substitute for real life, while the world went on without them. The more Andrea thought about it, the madder she got, and the more heavily she slammed the shovel into the earth.

Andrea's cracked and blistered hands screamed with every twist of the shovel. When finished, the hole would be wide and deep enough for each of them to crawl under, one after the other.

They were sweaty and dirty and tired, and almost out of Reverie for good.

The precise second Andrea scooped out the last bit of dirt they needed to get rid of in order to fit underneath, hope spread like a river through her body, tentative at first, then growing and swelling through all the parched, cracked places inside her. All of their work was about to be worth it. They were almost free.

Andrea turned to her brother and her new, old friend. She could see the other side of the hole they had created past the iron gate. Beyond the hole in the earth stood the dark and dense forest Andrea hoped would lead them all home. The three of them had entered Reverie at different times, but they would be leaving it together.

"No Sandman?" Andrea asked her brother, who was standing guard.

"No."

"Good."

"After you," Penny gestured to the hole in the ground, forcing a smile.

"If it's somehow . . . not what we hope on the other side," Andrea said, touching her raw and weary hand to Penny's shoulder, "we won't abandon you. We'll stick by you and make sure you're okay. Promise."

Penny looked down at the dirt. "I know." She reached her own hand up and squeezed Andrea's, a determined fire burning behind her tired eyes. "I believe you."

"Are we ready?"

Francis, Andrea, and Penny all turned to the lights of Reverie, taking it in one final time. The shops, the heavy full moon, the Dream Clock tower, and a peek of the carousel at the end of the lane, where the fairway opened up to the square.

"We're ready," Francis said, almost at the same time as Penny.

"No matter what happens," Andrea said to Penny, "I'm glad I met you. And I'm glad to call you a friend."

Penny's dirt-stained cheeks flushed pink and she broke

out in a big smile, a spread of joy taking over her entire face. She wrapped Andrea up in the biggest, tightest hug.

"I feel exactly the same," she said as she finally pulled away. "Penny Periwinkle. Remember that, Andrea Murphy. In case we're separated and you ever need to find me."

"Got it," Andrea said.

Andrea went first, shimmying her body through the hole and leading the way for Francis to follow. Penny took up the rear. Andrea's pulse quickened and her hands broke out in a sweat, stinging the places where her digging had broken the skin. As she went, she imagined exiting the other side and running from the gates of Reverie into the dark woods. Connecting with the path that would lead her home. Maybe sending a message back through the fence for the other kids. Maybe Penny would still be with them and would have to figure out a way to navigate life in the world long after she left it. Or maybe Penny would exit the tunnel in 1956, and Andrea and Francis would find their way home without her.

She pulled herself out, immediately reaching back down to help Francis. Penny shimmied out shortly after.

The three friends stood, then froze in their places. The sound of Andrea's heartbeat thrashed inside her ears like a bass drum.

Francis pressed himself tightly to his sister.

A low, sinister laugh filled the air, and someone—maybe Penny—screamed.

They weren't staring at a dark, dense forest, the gates of Reverie behind them.

They hadn't crawled their way to freedom.

The hole had let them out facing the center of Reverie.

Directly in front of the fairway.

Still trapped inside.

THE OLD MAN ON THE DREAM CLOCK

Andrea crawled through the hole again and disappeared, only to reappear back inside Reverie a few seconds later. Again. And again.

Francis and Penny sat, backs hunched against the locked gate.

"I don't understand," Andrea said, glaring at the useless pile of dirt, angry at their role as pawns in the Sandman's messed-up game. "There has to be a way to get this to work."

"He has magic, Andrea," Penny said, her voice flat. "There's no way to beat it."

Andrea dragged herself out of the hole one final time and kicked the shovel. It skidded a few feet in the dirt, but mostly the hard metal sent a shooting pain through Andrea's foot. The icing on this horrific, never-ending cake.

Penny was right. They were all trapped there by magic; no attempt to break through on their own was going to work. Heat rose in Andrea's cheeks. How could she have thought she had even the remote possibility of helping them escape, or that she might be a match for the Sandman's enchantments? She should have remembered the utter wastefulness of giving in to hope.

Her brother stared at her with eyes that pleaded for answers Andrea couldn't give. She turned away from him and the trust embedded in his gaze and glanced up at the Dream Clock.

The stupid Dream Clock. With its picture of an old, friendly-looking man in a nightcap. The person no one had ever seen. "What are you looking at?" Andrea yelled at the only other adult face she had found here outside of a dream tent. "Smiling down at all of us like we should be having the time of our lives!"

He looked so different from the Sandman they knew, who watched without being seen and who played tricks and who believed it was somehow better to keep children inside. Andrea didn't even know if the man on the clock had ever existed, but he was as good a target as any to shoot her arrows.

"I don't have many answers." Penny stood and dusted the dirt off the front of her dress as best she could. "But there's something that might help. A place. A place I've never been able to quite understand on my own. I go there often, whenever the night starts to feel too long. And it has to do with the man on the clock. I think there's something there. Some clue hidden somewhere about what's really going on in this place. I can just feel it. And maybe together we can figure it out."

Andrea didn't know how the old man on the clock could possibly untangle Reverie's puzzle and help get them free, but she also didn't have any better ideas. They had hit a literal dead end. She had failed her brother at finding a way home, and they were completely trapped in the nightmare that was supposed to be a beautiful escape. Andrea was soul-starved for some proof that all her hope hadn't been in vain. If she didn't try something else soon, she might just break down in front of Francis. And she definitely couldn't do that.

"Fine," Andrea said, without much hesitation. "Let's go." If there was anyone besides the Sandman who knew where Reverie's secrets were kept, it was Penny. And maybe she was right. If there was a clue there, maybe they could figure it out together.

Penny's face gleamed, a bit more subdued than before, but almost as it had when they first met and Andrea agreed to learn Reverie's ropes by following her lead.

"We'll make a plan there, won't we, Drea? We'll figure it out. We'll come up with a plan," Francis said, his voice a little softer and a little less certain with each word.

Andrea fought to push back the incessant burning behind her eyes. She stared, unblinking, at the moon in an attempt at distraction. She let the light dry any hint of tears away.

It wasn't as easy as it had been before. The pressure continued to build behind her eyes, and in another place, too. Pressure built up inside her cracked heart, hot and churning like the summer air before a bad storm. The kind of storm that could produce a tornado. She touched her hand to her chest and pressed her fingers firm against it, as if she could somehow hold herself together.

Andrea couldn't promise much, but she promised as much as she could. "Yeah, buddy," she said, giving a squeeze to his shoulder. "We're going to try."

Francis walked between Andrea and Penny. Both girls kept a sharp eye on the crowds for any signs of a Margaret Grace or the Sandman, or any hint that his unseen eye was still on them.

"Should we tell the others?" Penny whispered to Andrea as they walked.

Andrea scanned the crowd of revelers. The tired eyes, the laughing, the bursts of energy as they ran from tent to tent.

If they spread the word that kids had been trapped here for years and years before they had a plan to defeat the Sandman and his magic, Reverie would turn into a world of kids filled with agony and fear and sorrow. There couldn't be much good in that.

"They'll need to know," Andrea whispered back. "But let's figure out what we're doing first." *If* they could figure out what they were doing. If their future was something more than melding into the crowds of Reverie children forever, destined to wander the lanes, un-aging, until the end of time.

As they passed the locked Dream Bank, Andrea imagined the billions and billions of grains of sand piled high inside the tower, a few precious grains of which she held in a vial in her pocket from the night the Sandman took her brother away. She scowled at the kind face of the man on the Dream Clock, at how he winked down at the children, looking like the kind of fellow who would be good at reading a bedtime story. Who wouldn't enjoy seeing a child sad. If he did exist, he sure wasn't helping them get home, which made him almost as bad as the Sandman himself.

Penny took them down a lane that started off like all the others but quickly took a different form. The tents grew spaced apart and dirty, with streaks of gray and brown instead of white and blue, like Reverie had wrapped them in camouflage, trying to blend them in until they disappeared. Empty cups, lollipop sticks, and cotton candy cones from the fairway piled up around them. Andrea couldn't imagine wanting to go inside one.

"A lot of kids think these tents, this old part of Reverie, is broken," Penny said, glancing behind them. "And the rest don't come this way because it doesn't look fun."

Despite herself, Andrea's stomach fluttered. If the Sandman, who was behind everything in Reverie, went to such trouble to make this lane so unappealing, then maybe there *was* something of value here, hidden away.

Francis must have thought the same thing, because he gripped Andrea's hand, and his dreamy eyes danced with mischief. It was the same look he had when they stayed up later than they should, reading stories by flashlight. Or when he woke up hungry in the middle of the night and they snuck downstairs for a midnight snack.

Andrea brought her free hand up to cover her nose as the stench of rot surrounded the final tents in the lane, like the garbage bin in her mom's garage the night before she pulled it to the curb. Maybe even worse. If the nightmares broke free from the confinement of their tents, Andrea bet this was where they would come to hide. Strange birdcalls and wolf howls echoed around them from every direction, and a sour wind wrapped around Andrea, coiling tightly enough to take her breath away before finally letting go. Francis pulled in close, clinging to Andrea's arm. She would have turned back if Penny hadn't led them here.

The lane narrowed, and the tents gave way to gnarls and knots of thorny bushes and vines. They closed in around them as they walked, while indecipherable panicked whispers blew past in a chilled breeze.

"I'm sorry," Penny said softly. "It's the only way to get there, but we've almost made it."

Andrea turned her body sideways to fit through the small open space, but still a thorn here and there caught her skin even through her clothes. At least Francis had more room for error. He was still so small.

"Just . . . a little . . . bit . . . farther." Penny squeezed through a nearly impossible narrow opening and disappeared from their sight. Andrea followed, one final thorn pricking her left shoulder before she broke free.

Despite its forsaken surroundings, the space itself emanated magic. Pulsed with it, radiating a quiet, golden light. The scent of lavender and vanilla seeped out between several stilled-but-once-spinning rides, including a warped Ferris wheel and a small train, rusted on its track. All long abandoned and creaking in the wind, their fallen-off pieces littering the dirt. A thick wall of fog surrounded the grounds, so dense they couldn't see beyond it, like they were standing in the middle of a cloud in the night. Or at the edge of the world.

So there had been more rides in Reverie than the lonely carousel in the center square. Still were, technically speaking, but they were here, broken and hidden away, tucked in at the end of a lonely row and a path crowded with thorns.

"I'm going to show you my favorite place in all of Reverie," Penny said. "But first, you've told me your story. I want you to know my story, too." She turned her head, taking in the space around them. "I want you to know why I came to this secret place so many times during what I thought was one long night."

Penny glanced behind them at the path of thorns, as if to make sure they were still alone. They were, but she lowered her voice anyway.

"When I came here, the Sandman found me and offered to make me a special wish." She paused a moment, taking a deep breath and exhaling it slowly. "I came here to forget my loneliness, so I asked for a dream filled with people who wanted to be my friend."

Andrea thought back to the boy Penny had called out to when they first met. How she pretended she had so many friends. And Penny's sad, lonely face when Andrea left her behind the first time. Her desperation when Andrea left her yet again after her confrontation with the Sandman. Looking back, it was as obvious as the full moon above them in the inky sky.

She opened her mouth to speak, but Penny was quick to continue, almost rushing her words, like she would burst from the inside if they didn't find a way out.

"Making friends was difficult for me back home. The kids at school called me all sorts of names. I don't look like the girls in the movies. I get too excited. I cling too close." Penny squinted, her eyes fogged over, reliving a memory neither Andrea nor Francis could see. "Reverie came to me on the day of my birthday party. We had fruit punch and cake and cookies on a picnic table in my backyard. And no one came."

Andrea placed a gentle hand on Penny's arm.

"I left my house, ignoring my mother's pleas to stay and talk. I walked to the park and found a path I hadn't noticed before in the trees. As I walked, day turned so quickly into night. The sky took on a hint of pink, then deepened to orange, then to purple. And I found the ticket booth and Margaret Grace and this incredible circus. She didn't have to spend much time at all convincing me to come inside.

"Once in, the Sandman gave me what I asked for as my wish. In my special tent I had so many friends. But something wasn't quite right. They were all cold to the touch. They weren't real. They didn't like me because they *chose* to. They liked me because that was what they were made to do."

"I know that feeling," Francis said. "The Sandman made me a tent of my family all together, just like in my favorite pictures. But maybe I said my wish wrong, because what I meant was that I wanted a tent where I could *be* in our family. Only when I went into what was supposed to be my perfect wish, every room already had a Francis. They didn't need another one. No one even noticed." His voice lowered, laced with heartache. "No one knew I was there."

Andrea grabbed hold of Francis's hand.

"He's tricky, isn't he." Penny hugged her arms around herself. "And when I left my wish tent, all that time spent with all those friends inside it didn't make it any easier for me to make real friends out here. It felt like I was promised something real and given something as fragile as paper."

Penny scanned the rides as the fog curled around them. "So I became determined to learn everything about Reverie that I could. I thought if I became an expert, maybe someone would find me useful, at least, and then I could be with real people and I wouldn't be alone. Even for a little while." She sighed. "That's how I found this. There was something about the magic in this place. Something about the ride I'm about to show you with the man on the clock. It's helped me clear my head of the darkness that sometimes gathers during my stay. There are answers here about this place, I just know it. Even if I haven't been able to find them yet. And it's my favorite because it helps me remember that Reverie really is good. Or at least, it *was*, once upon a time."

Francis reached up, touching Penny's arm. "Thank you for telling us your story, Penny."

Penny brought a hand to Francis's cheek. "Thank you for telling us *yours*."

"Yeah," Andrea shifted her weight, forcing herself to look in Penny's eyes. Apologies had never come easy. "I'm sorry I abandoned you before . . . both times."

Penny shrugged and gave a small smile. "It's okay. You're here now. And maybe my problem isn't that I can't make friends." She took hold of Andrea's and Francis's hands, forming them into a circle. "Maybe I just hadn't met the right ones yet."

Andrea squeezed Penny's hand, and Francis squeezed hers. Acknowledging a mistake she had made and knowing she was forgiven filled in another missing piece inside her heart. She still didn't have the solution, but at least she wasn't lost in Reverie alone. She had her brother, and she had her new friend Penny. It had been a long time since friendship had come easily for Andrea, too. She hadn't recognized it at the time, but trying to protect a fragile heart by pulling away from the world led to a very lonely life. This small, special circle here with her now gave Andrea the confidence she needed to believe that they'd find a way to figure this out. Hopefully very soon.

"Now, come on." Penny let go of their hands and led them up to a massive ride. The front of the ride, built of curved metal, stood almost two stories tall. Images popped off the background in lifelike bumps and waves. The picture of a puffy, blue cloud with eyebrows, eyes, full cheeks, a nose, and a mouth blowing wind filled the left side. The swirling white trails of the wind formed the middle. The image of a world filled the right, an island floating in the sky, with striped tents, and a clock, and pops of bright color throughout. *Reverie.* And floating above the island was the image Andrea had seen so many times over however long she'd been here. The image of the Sandman. The friendly one, in his pajamas. In the picture, he descended down into the world of Reverie with a wink and a smile, his umbrella held out proudly above his head like a parachute, dropping him down to his home.

The sign above the ride read, in wide, blue, puffed-out print: *The Inception of a Dream.*

"This way." Penny walked them around to the side, where a small river flowed, its bottom formed by light blue concrete.

The river started out of their sight back in the wall of fog and flowed straight into the darkness of the ride itself.

"Are you ready?" Penny asked, clearly pleased with herself.

"Ready," Andrea said.

Francis nodded.

Penny grabbed hold of a tarp to her left and lifted it, tossing it aside. Beneath the tarp stood a long lever, stuck into the earth like the one that opened Reverie's gates. Penny widened her stance and held on to the lever, rocking back on her heels and tugging it toward her, trying to work it loose. "Here . . . we . . . go!"

The lever released, sending Penny back into the dirt like a shot. Francis bolted to her, but Penny was up and laughing within seconds of her fall. "Every time," she said, dusting off her bottom. "Every single time."

The entire ride sprung to life. A warm light wrapped around all that had once been covered in shadow. The cloud slipped into motion on the blue background, shifting back and forth and blowing a now waving wind. The old man descended, lower and lower, toward Reverie. The lights below him twinkled, awaiting his arrival into the circus world.

A silver rowboat made its way through the river, stopping in front of where they stood and waiting for them to board.

Andrea was so ready to find out whatever it was about

this ride that would, as Penny said, remind them that Reverie was meant for good and teach them about the man on the clock.

They stepped onto the boat and took their seats. Penny sat alone in the front row, and Andrea and Francis sat together in the back as the boat pulled them gently into *Inception of a Dream*.

INCEPTION OF A DREAM

The boat hitched onto a ramp that pulled them up a steep hill. Pulled them higher than the ride had looked from the outside. But Andrea was done being surprised at the way Reverie played with space and time. Entire worlds were contained inside small circus tents. Children had disappeared from their homes and been gone for decades. A ride could appear to be a certain height and yet not be bound by it.

The boat leveled out at the top of the ramp and began a smooth and slow descent. A dim scene appeared in front of them, with animatronic-looking children whose eyes blinked and whose arms lifted up and down. Francis slid close to his sister. Andrea wrapped her arm around him and squeezed it tight. The warmth of his body met hers and pushed straight through to her core. No matter what happened at the end of all this, it felt *so good* to be able to hold him again. To protect him when he felt scared.

In the first scene, a single spotlight shone brightly on a forlorn child's face. The walls behind him wept with tears. The light went out, then turned on another child, this time a girl, clutching a ragged stuffed animal, tears soaking the front of her dress. Then she, too, went dim. The lights flashed on more and more children, slowly at first, then picking up speed until they illuminated an entire chorus of children before the crying wall. They represented all the cultures of the world and all the great sadnesses of life. Loneliness, grief, hunger, poverty, fear, chains, a bridled mind, physical pain, misunderstanding. They had all lost sight that goodness exists, and they lived in the darkness of despair.

Andrea wouldn't have been surprised if the light had flashed on her own face, and Francis's, and Penny's. Her face could have easily joined in with the faces of all the children from all walks of life who had experienced things that shook them to their core and grated down their sense of hope. Things that were responsible for causing some people's hearts to grow frail and fragile. To crack. The reasons some chose to turn away from their sorrow and run.

Above them, almost hidden by a cloud, was the man from the Dream Clock. His own face twisted in sorrow, and tears poured freely from his eyes, as swift and heavy as rain, like he couldn't stand to see the children suffer.

The scene went dark, and they floated slowly through an arched opening carved into craggy rock like the entrance to a cave, as empty and as dark as the center of the earth. Or the blackness of night before the first hint of dawn.

The next scene sprung to life. Andrea recognized some of the faces from the first—the children who had shed rivers of tears. In this scene, each child slept.

Their chests rose slowly, up and down. Each child rested, suspended from the branches of gnarled, ancient trees on golden hammocks. The hammocks gently swayed, and a lullaby built of the hum of crickets, and the wind in the leaves, and an owl's song tucked tightly around them like a blanket.

The old man looked down upon them, and the rain from his tears pooled together, then turned into wisps of smoke that morphed in color and shape, light and shadow. The smoke lifted higher and higher, gathering itself together where the night sky met the heavens above the sleeping children's heads.

Building into something.

An island in the sky.

Then this scene, too, went dark.

The current picked up its pace, and their descent grew steeper, ushering the boat faster now into the next room.

In this one, the Sandman, as he appeared on the Dream Clock tower, floated down into a recognizable Reverie via his dream umbrella, with a face so filled with compassion, Andrea couldn't stand to stare at it too long.

A crowd of children gathered outside Reverie's gates. With a wink and a smile, the Sandman opened the gates and the animatronic children, once so, so sad, rushed through, their faces filled with wonder and excitement and relief.

Andrea understood now. Penny had been right when she said Reverie *was* good. Reverie was created to help alleviate the sadness of the children of the world. To give children a release from their sorrows and their pain.

Then somehow it had turned into a nightmare.

The lights of the scene faded, plunging the boat once more into darkness. Andrea, Francis, and Penny fell off the edge of a waterfall they couldn't see. Andrea's stomach dropped, and she held on to Francis with all her might.

All three of them screamed.

And then . . . it was over. The boat leveled out as they entered one final cave, filled with a luminescent glow.

Penny giggled and turned to them with a face that said she knew the drop was coming and had chosen not to warn them.

Andrea glared back at her but turned her lips up at the

edges. Francis lifted his small sweet face and smiled, too.

They were safe.

The current propelling the boat forward slowed, quiet now, and patient. Taking its time.

A smaller version of the Dream Clock stood in the middle of the cave, the tip of its tower pricking the ceiling. The single hand on the clock had barely crossed over into *Awake*, and it began to chime.

The animatronic children gathered at Reverie's gate, and the old man, in his light blue slippers, nightgown, and cap, sang a most hopeful song. His voice was pure, and sweet, and like a man's but also like a boy's. A mix of age and innocence and goodness.

> "Return, dear ones, to where you came.
> May this sweet reprieve give you strength.
> Should your heart tomorrow be once more built of sorrow,
> Take comfort and here return once again."

The gate swung open as he sang, and his words wrapped around Andrea's heart like a long, full hug.

The scene went dim, and the boat floated them back out into the Reverie night air.

***

Andrea, Penny, and Francis sat down on the dirt as the boat drifted away on the river and disappeared into the wall of fog.

Reverie today was *so different* from the Reverie of this ride. This Sandman believed that things would get better. And he had helped make them better by offering the promise that no child suffering from sorrow need ever be alone.

Now, having gone through the ride herself, Andrea knew what Penny was talking about. There was something here . . . some sort of clue. They only had to figure out what it all meant.

"So the children used to be allowed to leave and the clock wasn't always frozen in place?" Francis asked, picking at a dead blade of grass.

"I think so," Penny said.

"Why did it stop moving?"

"I don't know." Penny sighed. "It's been that way since I got here. Until you two came along, I always thought it just moved really slowly, or that I had only been here a little while."

"There has to be a reason," Francis said.

"However awful he is, maybe the Sandman is right . . . maybe it really isn't *possible* for us to leave." Andrea's gaze locked on the tip of the Dream Clock in the distance. "Unless we find a way to unfreeze the clock."

"But how?" Penny rested back on the dirt and stared up at the stars.

Andrea had no idea. The tower was locked, so they had no way to get inside it. Even if they did, she didn't know anything about fixing regular clocks, let alone magic ones. Andrea joined Penny on the dirt, interlacing her fingers and drumming them on her chest.

Francis joined them, too, and they all rested in the silence. The silence of the calm before . . . before whatever it was that would come next. Something was coming. Andrea could feel it in the prickles of magic dancing on her skin.

She stared hard at the tiny dots of light above them. Hundreds and thousands of blinking stars. She thought back to the *Star Builder* tent and wondered if, in some way, the world of the dream was true, if that was really how the first stars in the universe joined into creation.

Where were she, Francis, and Penny now even in the midst of creation itself? Maybe they were on an island built of dreams, floating in the sky, like the ride suggested. Or maybe Reverie existed outside of time and space, and this was Reverie's own moon and its own stars—or universe, even. Her insides ached, both hollow and full at the same time at the thought. With her hopefully real brother beside her and her half-healed heart, so aware of how very far she was from home.

Francis spoke first, disrupting the quiet. "You know, I think it would be hard to go home at the end of the night, since the reason we all came here was because we were having a bad time in life."

"Yeah," said Penny. "But I think maybe it's supposed to be more of a break from the sadness, don't you, Andrea?" She looked over. "Like that was the whole point?"

"An escape," Andrea nodded. A break. A chance to recharge one's strength.

"Not a trap." Francis spoke, wistful, like he was missing something he never had the chance to really know at all: the true wonders of Reverie, the way it was meant to be.

Andrea knew the Sandman had lost his sister and that he tried to reason it was somehow better for children to stay, but Andrea couldn't wrap her mind around that moment of transition. When Reverie—the way it used to be—disappeared and the way it was now took its place.

And she couldn't figure out what would have happened if she had come to Reverie with everything still as it once was. If she had enjoyed Reverie for one single night, then gathered with the other children at the gates as the Dream Clock chimed and the old man sang them home. It would have been hard to return to real life. But the Sandman, at least the one on the ride, said the kids could come back if they needed it. It wouldn't have been goodbye for good.

A lump formed inside Andrea's throat, so big she almost couldn't swallow. Because, if she was completely honest with herself, she wasn't sure that knowing she could come back would have been enough to get her to leave. She had come to Reverie to run away, and she meant it. A nightlong escape would have been nice, but the morning light would have brought with it a harsh awakening if her own heart hadn't started to change.

And then.

Like the old man's tears floating up into the sky and forming themselves into a dream circus, Andrea's fluid, foggy thoughts shifted and solidified, taking on the shape of an idea.

What if there *was* a kid at some point? A kid who faced a great, great sadness and who couldn't bring himself to go back to a world he thought would bring only pain and suffering in the end.

"What if he isn't the Sandman?" Andrea asked, softly at first. Almost to herself.

"Hmm?" Penny asked.

Francis propped himself up on his elbows.

Andrea repeated it, louder, fully aware that the Sandman might be listening and not caring if he was. "What if the Sandman isn't the Sandman?"

Penny gave Andrea a questioning look.

"Listen," Andrea said, trying to catch enough thoughts inside her whirring mind to form them into sentences that Penny and Francis would understand. "He looks nothing like him. He says kids can't leave." She jumped to her feet and paced back and forth, picking up speed. "What if he was a Reverie kid who didn't want to go home? The story we saw in there—*Inception of a Dream*—the old man, Reverie, all of it. It's magic. It's timeless. The Sandman we know isn't timeless. He has a history, his own sad story on earth. His life was already hard, and then he lost his sister. So . . ." She stopped in front of them and set her hands on her hips, every muscle in her body taut. "What if he *isn't* the Sandman?"

Andrea held her breath while she waited, her own mind spinning, frenzied, and out of control.

"But the Sandman says he created this place," Francis said.

"But we also *know* he's a liar."

Penny pulled her eyebrows together. "Do you think that's really true?"

"I think it could be," Andrea said, biting her bottom lip. "Even if I'm wrong, what have we got to lose?"

Penny thought a moment more, then nodded and stood, her face resolute.

Francis stood, too, his features all scrunched together. "If it's true," he said carefully, as if sifting each and every word before it came out, "then what happened to the real Sandman? The old man on the Dream Clock?"

Penny gasped and clutched Andrea's wrist. "He didn't . . . murder him, did he?!"

Andrea's heart pounded. The Sandman they had come to know was a *man*. The real Sandman was magic. A being who had existed maybe forever and who had created Reverie for the benefit of children. If he had been murdered . . . well, then all would be lost.

She had to hope there would be a different ending to his, and their, story.

Andrea turned once more to the Dream Clock tower where it stood, as ever, in the distance. The tower that contained a broken clock, and a locked door that opened with a single black key, and an enormous supply of magical sand.

Sand powerful enough to put anyone into a deep and deathlike sleep.

The tower—the heartbeat of Reverie. Maybe the Sandman hadn't been referring to the tower itself, or even the dream sand, but to something else *inside* the tower when he had said it.

"I'm going to need you both to trust me," Andrea said. "In case he's listening. You need to trust that I have a plan."

Penny and Francis nodded. Hopefully they, too,

understood the importance of catching the Sandman, who-ever he really was, by surprise.

Andrea stuffed her hand in her pocket, clutching the small vial she had kept for so long. It was only a pinch, really. But it might buy them enough time to steal what they would need to set everything right.

Most of all, it might be their ticket home.

TO REMEMBER

Andrea, Francis, and Penny broke free of the knotted, thorny vines and bolted past the run-down Reverie tents, past the Dream Clock and the hordes of weary-eyed Reverie children, and down the lane that would lead them to the Sandman's private dream.

But there, where it should have been, stood a lonely stretch of empty, forsaken field.

The Sandman's tent was gone.

Francis crumpled on the ground like a pile of dirty laundry. "Now we'll never get home!" Tears brimmed in his eyes, spilling over and falling down his cheeks.

"This can't be right," Penny said, running into the empty space. "Where'd he go?"

Andrea bent down to comfort her brother, then walked to the place where the entrance to the tent should have been.

Francis was devastated, Penny was confused. But something like a thrill surged through Andrea at this development. She wasn't surprised that he knew they were coming. And if they weren't onto something, the Sandman would have had no reason to hide himself away. She also knew the Sandman would never in a million years abandon Reverie, which meant he still had to be around somewhere.

"One of the Sandman's first questions to me was if I had come to Reverie to remember or to forget," Andrea said.

"He asked me that, too," Penny said. "I said I wanted to forget my loneliness."

Francis chimed in. "I wanted to remember the good times when we were all together."

Andrea paused a moment. "I told him I came here to forget." Her gaze landed on her brother.

He wiped the stream of tears from his cheeks, watching Andrea with a curious expression on his face.

"I'm so sorry, buddy. It hurt so bad to have you gone."

Francis blinked, slow and thoughtful, before giving a slight nod. A quiet way to tell Andrea *I understand.*

The pressure inside Andrea's heart rose up again, then pinched a little, as she remembered how the Sandman had tempted her to forget her brother altogether.

That had never been what she wanted. She had only ever wanted to forget the pain.

If they were onto him, he probably would have hidden himself somewhere he thought Andrea would never go in a million years. He already knew she would go into the nightmares. He wouldn't have any reason to hide himself behind a good dream. She had gone into her memory of the night Francis disappeared, fueled by the fierce desire to find her brother, but the Sandman still thought she had come here to forget. Which meant that maybe the place he thought Andrea would never enter would force her to do the opposite: *To remember*. To enter a place so saturated with memories that she wouldn't be able to escape her sadness and her pain at all they had lost. A place where their entire family was together.

"I think I know where he is." Andrea knelt down by her brother and cradled his face in her hands. "Francis, do you think you can take us to the wish the Sandman created specially for you? The one with our family all together?"

A ripple of understanding passed over Francis's expression. "Oh yeah!" he said. "Let's go."

He stood, and Andrea placed her arm around Francis's shoulder. They walked in the direction of Francis's tent, while Penny lingered a few steps behind.

"Come on, Penny." Andrea turned back to her. She had

left Penny behind enough. She knew now how it had made her feel, and Andrea was determined not to abandon her friend again.

Penny's face lit up when Andrea stopped, her face reflecting the light of the moon before fading to a more serious expression.

"I think . . ." Penny said, slowing to a stop. "I think this part is something you and Francis need to do together. Just the two of you."

Andrea's chest deflated. "But, Penny, we need you. You've helped us with everything so far. I won't leave you behind." Andrea reached out her hand to Penny, but her friend stepped away.

"I know," she said. "That's the thing. I know you wouldn't leave me. And we'll meet again very, very soon. I still think there's a way I can help. A way I *should* help. It just means I have a different job right now than you do."

"We need to find the Sandman, Penny. *That's* our job."

"No. *You* need to find the Sandman . . . and I . . . I need to gather the others. We'll meet you at the Dream Clock."

Andrea shifted her weight, uncomfortable at the thought. "If we fail, you'll have gathered all the children together for nothing. They'll think you're a liar. No one will ever trust you again."

Penny smiled. "*When* you succeed, there won't be much time. They need to be there, waiting. They need to see how it ends so we can all go home."

As uneasy as it made Andrea, she realized that Penny was right.

"You're very brave," she said, wrapping Penny in a giant hug. It was true. Penny trusted Andrea and Francis enough to go off on her own to help them. She chose to believe that they would get the job done, so fully that she was willing to put herself on the line for it.

"I've decided that I'd rather be lonely in the real world than trapped in this fake one," Penny said.

And she was willing to return home, in spite of once being so desperate to leave it.

"Besides," she continued. "I got my wish. I found real friends."

Penny mussed Francis's hair.

He blushed and looked to the ground.

"See you later, alligator. Take care of your big sister."

Francis nodded. "I will."

"See you on the other side." Penny pivoted away, lifted her chin, and marched forward alone toward the Dream Clock.

Andrea took a deep breath, an attempt to slow her pounding heart. She could never go back to the blind joy she had felt during her first moments inside Reverie's gates, when she thought she could run away from her troubles. So many things had changed, and, one way or another, they were about to change again.

If they succeeded, Andrea wasn't sure she was ready to return to a world where she might wake up without a brother. But for now, she just had to take the next step, which was to find the Sandman.

And to find him, they had to confront Francis's perfect wish.

UNBROKEN

Andrea and Francis walked down a lane of tents that emanated possibility and potential. The air sat as heavy and still as the moment before bright candles on a birthday cake are extinguished with a single breath. *One More Day with You, The Endless Before, Unbroken*—even the tents themselves pulsed with all the wishing.

Francis stopped in front of *Unbroken*, and Andrea pulled in alongside him. Here it was. The perfect wish the Sandman had created just for Francis. A wish he could have stayed in forever, if he chose to. And there, attached to it, stood the sweeping black-and-white-striped tents of the Sandman's private dream. Exactly as Andrea had predicted.

It should have been satisfying, figuring out where the Sandman had hidden himself away. But fire burned in Andrea's eyes as she acknowledged the truth: the reason she knew he would hide here behind Francis's tent had more to do with the similarities between the two of them than any sort of difference. They did it in their own ways, but both she and the Sandman were experts at avoiding confrontation of their loss. And he didn't think she would ever confront the fullness of hers by walking through this tent.

Francis fiddled with the fabric of his pajama top. "It's going to be hard to go through it."

"I know." Andrea closed her eyes, soaking in the blackness. "There's so much that I've tried to forget." And there was. Until Reverie, she had never succeeded in forgetting anything, but it never stopped her from trying to find different ways to escape.

"No, that's not it," Francis insisted. "*I* wanted to remember, and now we're trying to leave. This is the last time I get to see our family together. I have to say goodbye."

The pain in Andrea's heart surged once more from deep, deep inside her. This was exactly what she had tried to protect herself from. It was why she had run away from so many things.

This tent would be difficult for both of them, but for very different reasons. And there was one extra piece for Andrea that Francis didn't know about. Couldn't know about. She was about to walk through a tent filled with moments of their family together, all with her lost brother by her side.

A brother she couldn't be sure was real but was still desperately trying to save.

∗∗∗

Andrea and Francis stood in their old backyard in the first scene of Francis's dream. Andrea stared hard at a family, at *her* family, playing on the swing set. A younger version of herself climbed the stairs to the play set's wooden tower. Her mom carried out a tray of lemonade and set it on a table. Her dad smiled as he pushed a young Francis on a swing.

"There you go, champ," he said, his voice swelling with pride. "Keep pumping those legs!"

No one in the dream family could see them. Andrea reached for Francis's still warm hand and squeezed. Something about this scene tickled at the corners of Andrea's mind as they watched it play. She recognized this moment. Four, five summers ago, maybe. Andrea was seven, Francis was four. Her parents had surprised them with a swing set, just to make them smile. Andrea remembered thinking even at that age how long they must have saved up to get it.

It was one of the pictures Francis kept on his dresser and had arranged so carefully. One of his prized possessions come to life.

They watched until the living memory grew hazy before

their eyes. The dream family took on a translucence, slowly fading, disappearing again into the sands of time. She watched until she could barely make out their forms, could barely hear Francis's squeals as their father pushed him higher and higher on the swing. They watched until they were gone.

This was an irreplaceable moment in their lives that they would never experience again. Part of the empty space inside her heart, the vacuum created by all the things they'd lost.

"This way." Francis led Andrea to the house, which they entered through the back screen door. Inside, they found much the same as they had in the first scene. Each room contained a memory. In the dining room, her dad carved a small turkey on Thanksgiving while they all waited for him to dish out their servings, their eyes gleaming at the abnormally abundant spread. The aroma of potatoes and spices wafted in the air. Another one of Francis's pictures. He had asked the Sandman to build him an entire tent of the pictures he had so lovingly kept to help him remember.

When the family before them faded, Andrea and Francis entered the living room, into a scene set in the aftermath of Christmas morning. Wrapping paper wreckage framed carved-out spaces for a two-year-old Francis to push a new digger truck and for a five-year-old Andrea to work out a puzzle in a room perfumed by tape and pine.

Her parents sat on their worn-out floral couch with messy bedheads of hair and tired but content expressions on their faces. Then they, like the others, also faded away.

Andrea and Francis climbed the matted gray carpet on the stairs and peeked into her parents' room, right at the top. Through the crack in the door, the four of them snuggled on the bed, reading bedtime stories, and Andrea caught a whiff of mintberry toothpaste in the air. A stack of books rested on the nightstand next to her dad. The dream children's eyes grew heavy as they listened to their father's calm, mesmerizing reading of *Owl Moon*. They were older in this one. They had taken a selfie that night, their parents sticking smiles on their faces because Francis begged them for a picture. They smiled for him, even though they weren't really happy, and Francis had printed it out on their home computer. This picture was taken only days before their parents split. Days before Francis disappeared.

Andrea pushed the door open to step inside, and her heart filled with so much longing she thought it might explode. She wanted to crawl right in alongside the family, to smell her mother's perfume and her dad's cologne and to feel the fluffy, warm covers she had snuggled in and napped in so many times when she was young. She stood there for a moment, pretending the family didn't actually consist of dream stuff, that they weren't about to fade away. That she could take her rightful place between them and stay somewhere they had never grown unhappy and had never lost Francis and where she wasn't stuck in this strange and terrible world.

"It's over," Francis said, his face shining with tears. "This is the last room of my wish."

Andrea's eyes burned so hard they could be on fire. Of course this was the end. This room was the scene from the final picture on Francis's dresser. From the last picture of their family all together. They had made it.

An ice-cold wind blew through the hollow place inside Andrea's heart, making its presence known before dying back down to a dull ache. It was so hard to remember, but in some strange way, it also felt *good*. Andrea understood her brother better now. It would have been hard for her to leave Reverie if she had still wanted to forget. It was going to be just as hard to leave knowing now what it felt like to remember. Remembering kept the memories and the people that meant the most to you close. Even though she missed so many things, Andrea was glad to see them, even if only in the moving picture of a wish come to life. And maybe the chance to remember the good times might, someday, make it easier to live with the missing. The ache, Andrea imagined, that might never quite go away.

"Uh-oh." Francis let go of her hand and walked toward

what Andrea assumed was the wish's exit, but she turned to find the color drained from her brother's face.

Francis's exhausted, worried eyes met his sister's. "That's not the normal door."

"What do you mean it's not the normal door?"

"This used to be the exit. It led me back to a lane of tents. I thought it would be replaced by the entrance to the Sandman's tent . . . but see," Francis pointed to the top of the wood. "It's got its own name."

Andrea's gaze followed Francis's finger. It was true. Carved into the door that once let Francis back out into Reverie, and that they hoped would lead them to the Sandman, was a single word: *Home*.

Magic and light seeped from the crack between the floor and the heavy wood. The air hummed and vibrated with it, tickling Andrea's cheeks. If felt somehow more potent than any of the other dreams she had been in. Except the Sandman's tent. The pull of this dream, the heaviness of it, felt a lot like the heaviness of the Sandman's private dream. Which had to mean they were close—to the Sandman, and to their chance to set things right. It also meant that whatever the Sandman had set up beyond this door was probably built to break them.

Andrea swallowed hard.

"You got a little more in you, buddy?" she asked, pulling her brother in beside her.

"Do you?" Francis stared, wide-eyed and vulnerable, at his sister. He was tired. She was tired. Andrea had to imagine this entire world of children also had to be tired.

Andrea nodded and clutched the handle, letting the light and magic surround her as they stepped through the door.

"HOME"

Andrea's eyes opened to a sky built of glow-in-the-dark stars. The weight of a comforter rested heavily on top of her. Yellow-green moonlight seeped into the room like smoke. It tucked itself into corners and crept up the bunk bed, spreading over Andrea like a cloud.

This was her room. This was her house. Set up to look like she had woken up in her bed, an echo of the tricks the Sandman had played on her before.

This was the final dream sequence on their way to the Sandman's tent. On their way to their final confrontation. Andrea was certain.

"Andrea?" Francis whispered. His soft voice sounded from beneath her on the bottom bunk.

"I'm here, buddy," she said, sitting up. Andrea swung her legs off the top and landed gently on the carpet.

Francis slid out and took Andrea's hand. The light swirled around them, caught up in a breeze from the window, tucking them inside it and leaving a thin glow.

Each dream she had entered in Reverie had been immersive, but they had never been like this. This time they weren't watching a dream or following along with a story as a set of dream characters led the way. This time, they *were* the dream. They were the main characters. This was their story.

A gentle song, its melody smooth and rich as velvet, flowed to their ears through the crack in their bedroom door. The tinkle of laughter rose above the music in a crescendo before dipping back down below the bass line.

Andrea's heart hurt a little bit harder at the thought of the unknown. Some part of it wanted her to stop. To go back in time and find a way to avoid having to confront whatever would meet them at the bottom of the stairs in case she couldn't take it. In case whatever came next was too much for her to bear.

But distraction and avoidance had only ever offered Andrea temporary relief. Her attempts at self-protection had never really helped her *through* anything. They had only made her stuck, tricked her into thinking she was fine.

If Andrea was completely honest, she had to admit that probably no one was supposed to always and at every moment be okay. She had seen how many children had come to Reverie, each one of them here because they needed a night of escape. There had been pain and sadness throughout the whole world and since the beginning of time. Maybe it wasn't so much about protecting herself from the pain anymore as it was learning how to walk through it. And allowing herself to heal.

The floor at the top of the stairs creaked as Andrea and Francis tiptoed toward the source of the sound.

The music came from the kitchen. And the laughter came from their mother. Their parents were together. They danced next to a darkened window, the dishes from dinner still piled up next to the sink.

Their father twirled their mother, then swayed. Step, step, back. Step, step, back. Andrea recognized the song. It was the same song her father had danced to with her, from when she was so small she had to stand on his feet and let him carry her through the house. Step, step, back. Step, step, back.

When the song ended, he pulled their mom in close for a hug. She pulled away after a moment, her eyes warm with love. And they leaned in for a simple kiss.

Their parents had always offered hugs and kisses to Andrea and Francis, but Andrea couldn't remember a time over the past many years when she saw her parents even holding hands, let alone being affectionate like this.

"Gross," Francis whispered. But when Andrea looked at Francis's face, it wasn't an expression of disgust that he wore. It was an expression of uncertainty and maybe a little bit of sadness.

"Oh, kids!" Andrea's mom caught them out of the corner of her eye and opened her arms, pulling them out of the hall-way's shadows. "You're supposed to be in bed." The words themselves should have been an admonishment, but her mother's mouth and eyes smiled, and she looked up at their father as if to say, *Well, what can we do?*

Andrea's dad nodded and moved to restart the song.

"One dance," her mom said. "Then back up to sleep."

Francis smiled. Andrea did, too, feeling her guard—and resolve—slip away. This moment felt *so good*, in fact, maybe the dream wouldn't be as bad as she thought. Maybe they could stay here for a little while. Their mission, whatever it was exactly, was important, but it would keep.

The music began again. Their dad danced with Andrea, and their mom danced with Francis, and the family spun together, slow and soft and smooth, the music flowing around them, the wooden floor creaking under their feet. Step, step, back. Step, step, back.

All of it, every single thing about this moment, felt so

incredibly *real*. The smell of her father's cologne, the stiff collar of his shirt. Her mother's hands resting on Francis's arm as they made slow circles in their moonlit kitchen. And, for whatever reason, maybe because of the extra magic at the heartbeat of this dream, they even felt warm to the touch.

Andrea could stay here forever.

"Should we tell them?" her father asked, his voice laced with excitement.

"I think now's a *perfect* time."

"Tell us what?" Francis asked, his eyes hopeful.

"You've woken up!" her mother said.

"Congratulations," her father patted Andrea and Francis on the shoulder.

"Wait . . ." Andrea paused. "What?"

"You've made it through, Andrea." Her mom bent down to Andrea's eye level. "You've brought Francis home. You've fixed things, just like you wanted."

Her father bent down, too. "Andrea, we're so proud of you. You've fixed *everything*."

Oh. Had she really fixed things?

The song ended, dropping off after one final, held-out note. The family stilled in the middle of the kitchen floor, with the crumbs hiding in the corners, and the dirty dishes, and the school papers stuck to the fridge with magnets.

"We . . ." their mother started.

Andrea's stomach twisted. She knew what was coming, but something didn't feel right. She just couldn't put her finger on it. These were the words their family used to say all the time when she was younger. It was the Murphy family anthem. It was said before bedtimes, and in silly moments, and in family hugs. It was said before all the sadness and the silence came between them.

"Are . . ." their father continued, his voice dragging the word out, prompting Andrea and Francis to join in what came next.

Though from a place deep inside her, storm clouds gathered, heavier and darker by the second, Andrea said the words without hesitation. Francis joined in, too, all four of them finishing the phrase together.

". . . a family."

Their mom and dad squeezed Andrea and Francis close, making a kid sandwich.

They said it again, her parents' voices both happy and resolute. Like it was an unchangeable truth. Like it would always be this way.

"We. Are. A. Family."

Andrea squished her eyes shut, trying to stop the fire burning behind them.

Something wasn't right. Andrea snuck a glance at Francis, who looked even more wrapped up in this moment than she was.

"Now, you two should run along to bed," her dad said. "We have a busy day tomorrow. Family breakfast, games . . . all the things you love."

"That sounds so fun!" Francis gave a little excited jump.

"And we'll do all of it together." Her mom touched the top of Francis's head. "Maybe even a trip to the park."

The park.

A swing set and river and an evil willow pretending to be kind. And a lost brother and lost years and a broken family in a shattered picture frame.

Andrea pinched her arm as hard as she ever had.

Nothing. Not a single ounce of sting.

The truth swept through Andrea like a gust of wind, clearing away the Sandman's mind fog. She pulled back from her dream parents. Because that's what they were: a heavy, potent dream.

"This isn't real," Andrea said.

Her dream parents placed protective arms around Francis.

"Andrea." Her mom gave a ragged, awkward chuckle. "Now don't be silly. We're together again. And it's time to go to bed."

"No." Andrea's words grew firmer, even more resolved.

"But you fixed things, Andrea!" Desperation ran through Francis's every word, enough to let Andrea know the magic's grip on her brother's mind had not yet taken a firm and final hold.

This was all too easy. It was too easy because it wasn't real.

Their parents stood and looked at each other one last time, their eyes so full of love, their hands still on Francis's shoulders.

"Oh dear," her father said. "Now look what you've done." In seconds the love in their eyes faded to harsh lines and hints of mistrust. Like the way they had looked at each other in the weeks before they split.

Their grip on Francis grew tighter, pinching, and Francis's face morphed from pleading to panic. Andrea lunged for her brother, wrapping her hands around her parents' wrists, which went from human and warm to ice-cold in a flash. Cold like all the other Reverie dreams. Their bodies turned to gray, then blue, exactly as they had when she thought *The Frigid Place* had followed her home.

Andrea jerked their hands upward, freeing Francis from their grip, and she and Francis both created as much distance from their dream parents as possible, pressing their backs up against the kitchen wall.

The kitchen cabinets grew visible through the once-solid

bodies of her parents as they slowly faded, mouthing angry words to each other that Andrea could no longer hear. The same kinds of words Andrea had fallen asleep to for so long before the house grew too still and too silent.

And then they were gone.

"No," Francis yelled, clawing the empty air. "No, no, no!" He tore around the kitchen, frenzied, as tears streaked down his cheeks. "Why did you do that, Andrea? Why did you send them away?"

"Because they weren't real," Andrea said softly. "Don't you see? He wanted to keep us here forever. He wanted to keep us in this dream so we'd never find our way home!"

"If this was a dream, then there would be a *door*. I don't see a door. Where's the door?!" Francis dragged his hands along the kitchen walls, peeling away some of the paint, then banged his fists against the thick glass windows, cracking one in the process.

"I don't know!" Andrea joined Francis in his fury, peeling more paint off the walls, trying to find the exit, fearing if she failed that she had doomed them to live alone in this empty dream house forever.

Andrea fell to the floor as each and every sadness whipped around inside her like a wild storm with deadly strikes of lightning and booms of thunder loud enough she thought she might shatter. All the things that had broken. The wholeness of their family. Her lost little brother.

She couldn't bring herself to keep looking for the door. The voice inside tempted her to walk back up the stairs and crawl into her bed, to let the dream start over and give her another chance to not send her parents away. The chance to live in a world where she could forget the reckless anger and the deep, deep pain she had carried for so long.

But Andrea had learned that she couldn't find the escape she had been hoping for in Reverie. She couldn't hide herself away in a dream. She couldn't run away from life forever. Even though she had lost the wholeness of her family, and even though it might mean she woke up without Francis.

Andrea was done pushing the heat back from behind her eyes and protecting what she thought was a fragile, near-broken heart. She was done avoiding the things that reminded her of all they had lost.

She was stronger than that now.

She was done running away from the pain.

The dream kitchen blurred in front of her, and out of Andrea's eyes poured milky, silver tears, like the mercury she had seen in her mom's old thermometer before they threw it away. She sobbed streams of them, rivers, oceans. They pooled around her on the floor of the kitchen, flooding the room and spilling out into the hallway with no hint of slowing down.

Francis paused his frantic searching, then waded over to her and put his warm arm around his big sister, comforting her, rubbing her back, letting her know he was there.

And, maybe most important of all, Francis let her cry.

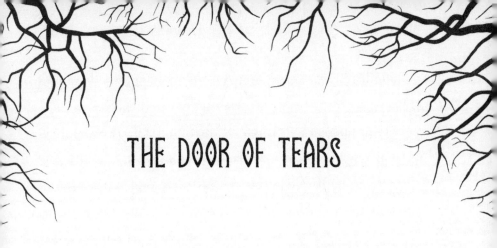

THE DOOR OF TEARS

Minutes, hours, eons later, and only once Andrea was emptied of all her tears, did something miraculous happen.

The silver tears stopped spreading around the dream version of their house. Each droplet changed direction and gathered inward, leaving dry spots on the floor, piling on top of each other and taking the shape of something solid. Something tall and rectangular, wavering but firm.

A door.

The door built of tears reflected the boy and girl who stood before it. Each with deep purple lines under their blood-shot eyes. Their hands entwined.

"Do you think it will take us to him?" Francis asked.

"The only way to know for sure is to walk through," Andrea said. If the Sandman went to all this trouble to hide himself away somewhere he never thought Andrea would go and to make a door out of tears she had said she'd never cry, he'd better be waiting for her on the other side. He meant for these dreams to break her. Though she did, in some ways, break, Andrea felt stronger than ever for having gone through it all.

She reached a tentative finger into the door, felt the water tickle at her skin, then pushed her hand in farther. Dry air greeted her on the other side. She stepped through, followed by Francis.

They arrived, dry and unharmed, in the middle of the Sandman's private dream. The room with the stage, where dream–Margaret Grace came to perform in front of nonexistent crowds. Where the lonely Sandman watched, unblinking, pretending his sister was still with him, even though he had created the lie of her himself.

The silhouette of the Sandman, with his pristine gray tuxedo and his plum hat, sat in the front row.

"I didn't think you would come." The Sandman stared straight ahead and spoke to them with a voice vacant of emotion. "I was sure you would choose to stay. If you'd like a different dream, Andrea, I trust that you still have the parchment. I can build you one that better suits you."

Andrea reached into her pocket and handed Francis the

object from inside it, motioning with her hands what she wanted him to do.

Francis nodded.

"My Margaret has just finished her show," the Sandman continued. "She'll be back soon, though, I assure you. Never before have you heard a voice so like the angels'."

"I know," Andrea said. She crept with light steps toward the Sandman while Francis did the same in the other direction. The pervading fog of the room wound around the chairs and the Sandman and the children. It rolled across the floor in choppy waves, licking Andrea's and Francis's ankles as they walked. "I've heard her sing."

"Isn't she magnificent?" the Sandman asked, his voice wavering, his eyes still fixed on the stage. Andrea had stepped in alongside him now and watched as a stream of tears shining bright as diamonds fell down his cheeks.

Andrea sighed. This man was awful, and wretched, and he had done some very terrible things. But he was also incredibly sad. The mystery and wonder she felt during their first encounter had long since faded, and pity now took its place.

"I've actually come to tell you I have chosen my dream," Andrea said, patting the folded parchment in her pocket. "I screwed up, I should never have sent that dream family away, but I'm ready now. You were right. Going through those dreams proved to me that I came here to forget. I *need* a place I can forget. If you're still willing to build it." Andrea's eyes no longer burned. They brimmed with tears, ready to fall freely. Francis's shadow danced behind the Sandman, moving closer, slowly and without sound.

The exit to the dream formed on the side of the tent.

The Sandman broke eye contact with the stage, landing his gaze on her. "Why yes," he said, his voice pleased, yet somehow also empty. "Of course. Who would want to live with so much pain?" He took note of the tears in Andrea's eyes as his fingers wrapped themselves tightly around his gray umbrella. "Oh yes, dear child. Draw it, and in moments you can forget all your sadness for good. Live in a world where your grief and sorrow never existed. No more tears. A forever escape."

Andrea moved her hand to her pocket, digging her fingers inside and grabbing hold of the paper.

Francis approached the Sandman from behind, cradling the final few grains of shimmering sand from Andrea's vial inside his open palm.

Francis's eyes met hers. He curled his fingers around the grains until his fingertips sparkled. Then he moved his hands in slow motion until they floated next to either side of the Sandman's head. He swept his hands over the front of the Sandman's face, sprinkling the sand into his unblinking eyes.

The grains soaked into the salty wetness of the Sandman's tears. He gasped and reached one hand up, clasping a strong, desperate grip on to Francis's wrist, but only for a moment. It soon fell limp beside him as his head slunk back and his jaw fell open, revealing two rows of perfectly white teeth. The dream sand speckled his face like fine sprays of paint. If his eyes had been open, they would have stared blankly at the ceiling of the tent.

But he wouldn't see the ceiling. Nor would he see Andrea as she peered into his face. He wouldn't see Francis bolt away to join his sister. He wouldn't see Andrea as she reached across the front row to swipe the precious gray dream-filled umbrella with its shining black key from his ice-cold hand.

No, he wouldn't see those things.

Because the Sandman had fallen asleep.

RACE TO THE DREAM CLOCK

"Quick—we don't have much time!" Andrea shouted as she and Francis broke free of the Sandman's tent. Andrea clutched the Sandman's umbrella in her white-knuckled hand. It hadn't been much sand. It wouldn't keep him asleep for long. Only a few minutes at most.

They made a run for the Dream Clock, where Andrea had to hope the Reverie children would have gathered with Penny's help, given that she and Francis now ran through empty lanes, the entrances to the tents flapping in the breeze with no children to rush inside them.

Andrea's heart skipped a beat when the voice of the Sandman, harsh and angry and sharp as a razor blade, shouted at them only seconds after they had turned the first corner. He had to know where they were going. Andrea took a quick pivot down a different lane to try to throw him off. If he caught them before they got there, if he was able to grab his umbrella, all would be lost.

A great roar sounded, like the sudden tearing of something large and thick. It filled the empty lanes, sending a ripple of wild wind past Andrea and Francis as they ran. The ground rumbled beneath their feet, and the dream tents shook from the bottoms up. A few seconds later another violent tear blasted their ears. Black smoke flooded the lane like a broken dam.

"Andrea, what's happening?!" Francis's pupils shrunk to the size of a pin, but his little legs continued to run. Andrea's did, too. Even when the shaking threw them off balance, they joined their hands together and kept moving forward.

The black smoke transformed into shapeless shadows, which gathered and roared and stank of rot and death. A bloodcurdling screech sounded, so close it shook the brains inside Andrea's head.

More tearing followed, the shock waves of each rip sending fierce gusts through the air.

Andrea and Francis scanned each tent as they ran past, finding that some had split apart, a mess of jagged tears in the canvas and splayed-open seams.

"Andrea . . ." Francis said, slowing down to a stop, his face deathly pale. Smoke collected around them, filling in the gaps between the tents.

Andrea tugged her brother forward, but it was as if his feet had turned to cement.

"The ripping sounds," he said, his voice forced and too quiet. "This lane. The tents that are broken. They're not the good dreams."

"What does that mean?!" Andrea snapped her head left and right in the gathering darkness. A group of shadows formed itself into a ghostly set of people, blocking the path Andrea and Francis had intended to take. One of them stepped forward, a woman with greenish skin and frizzed, knotted, sand-colored hair.

"Can you help me?" she asked. The woman, her eyes frenzied and beady, moved in uncomfortably close. Andrea scowled and backed away as the scent of swamp and pea soup crowded her, and the woman leaned in closer.

"I . . . I don't know how," Andrea pleaded, jerking Francis behind her.

The woman's face froze, each and every muscle paralyzed behind her sickly skin. She bared her yellow, jagged teeth, pressing them tight together and grinding them slowly, back and forth, back and forth. Andrea reached up to cover her ears from the grating sound, but she couldn't make herself look away. The woman didn't blink, didn't breathe. She just ground her teeth together, back and forth, back and forth, until they shook and fell from her mouth, the yellowed bits of bone clinking to the ground and bouncing away.

Andrea screamed.

With his umbrella, the Sandman had the power to release dreams from their tents, often setting them up as a show in the square for the delight of the Reverie children. Now, without it, the Sandman had improvised, opting to play yet another dark and dangerous game.

In his anger, he had torn open the tents containing nothing but horrors for the children who ventured inside them.

He had set the nightmares free.

***

Francis yanked on Andrea's arm, breaking her focus away from the horrible woman and pulling his sister back down the nightmare lane.

Black dust rolled through the air like tumbleweeds before disappearing into the shadows. Up ahead a gray cloud gathered, raining down a glittering substance.

Francis's eyes turned from fear to awe. "Snow," he said, his voice filled with wonder. He moved toward it with an expectant smile on his face, like he always did when the first sign of winter showed up each year.

It did look so, *so* pretty. Andrea and Francis moved to the cloud as if hypnotized and in slow motion. The cloud pushed, ever so slightly, toward them, beckoning them to step underneath it. Urging them to touch it. To catch a drop of snow on their tongues.

Andrea reached the cloud first. She held out her hand, the tip of her pointer finger crossing the barrier into the snow. A jolt of pain seared it and bolted up her arm. Deep red blood gathered on its tip, at the spot where the snow had cut her.

She jerked her finger away. Why would the snow hurt her? The pretty, pretty snow.

Francis reached his arm up toward the cloud.

"No—Francis!" Andrea caught her brother's arm just in time.

She showed him her finger. Francis shook his head, snapping out of it, then stepped back and out of the cloud's reach. There, on the ground, gathered thousands and thousands of razor-sharp snowflakes made of glass. The air around them filled with the light clinking of the flakes as they landed and shifted on top of each other. If they had stepped under the cloud, she and Francis would both have been cut in a million places while under the snow's spell.

Just then a bracing wind brought with it the scent of mystery and twilight and secrets whispered in the dark. *The Sandman.*

"Give me back my umbrella!"

Andrea reached her free hand into the pile of glass snow and grabbed a handful, ignoring the stinging as hundreds of tiny snowflake points sliced thin cuts into the palm of her hand. She pulled her arm back and threw the snow at the shadowed figure of the Sandman as he jumped out from around a corner.

He raised his arm up to protect his face as the snow slashed at his coat sleeves, buying them just enough time.

Andrea and Francis sprinted farther down the darkened lane.

Almost relieved, Andrea turned to get her bearings when a horrible laughter bubbled out at them from the shadow of a tent. From the darkness, a clown, the painted colors on his face cracked in jagged, crusted lines, leapt out at them. His frozen red smile smeared like blood across his cheeks and chin. In his hands he held a knife stained the color of rust.

"Time to play . . ." he uttered, his eyes hungry and his breath reeking of decay.

Andrea held fast to the umbrella as she pulled Francis between two tents, then onto the adjacent lane, hoping in vain that the nightmares wouldn't be able to follow. They darted through spectral figures with missing heads and blackened hearts. The heat of dragon's fire singed their heels. Graves opened up beneath their feet. A cloud of screaming bats, so thick they had to stop and hide their faces, nipped at their hair before ascending back into the night.

After all their running, the Dream Clock stood as a pinprick on the Reverie horizon past the wall of pervading nightmare fog. Andrea's chest grew tight, but they couldn't stop. Couldn't stay still. Because if the Sandman didn't find them, then the nightmares would swallow them whole.

Without a word the two children picked up their pace, faster and faster, though their clothes grew slick with sweat, their legs grew heavy as if they had actually turned to stone, and the nightmares clawed at their ankles. They only hoped they could stay enough ahead of the nightmares to make it in time.

Soon Andrea and Francis emerged from a wall of blackness and back into the center of Reverie and its clear night air.

The Reverie children watched them, creeping out around corners and staring with curious expressions and those dewy, exhausted eyes. Relief rushed through Andrea at the sight of them. Penny had succeeded. And so had they.

The black smoke hovered and hung and curled around the tents, and shrieks and wails still echoed around them, but the nightmares did not come near the Dream Clock with the heartbeat of Reverie inside it.

Still, Andrea's hand slickened with sweat as she clenched the gray umbrella in a grip as tight as death. Because in front of the heavy metal door to the Dream Clock tower, the Sandman stood in wait, a wicked smile on his hideous face.

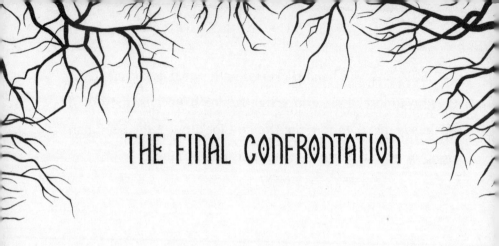

THE FINAL CONFRONTATION

Calm and still and smiling, the Sandman tucked his hands behind his back like he had yet another trick up his sleeve.

"Andrea and Francis," he began. "Never before have I had a pair of children give me so much trouble. And after all I've done for you." He turned to the rest of the children. "For *all* of you. I should have the nightmares devour you." He licked his lips. "Gobble you up."

The nightmares continued to fill in the shadows behind them but remained clear of the square. Andrea found Penny's face at the front of the crowd of children that now gathered, forming a tight semicircle around Andrea, Francis, and the Sandman. Children from all over the earth who had no idea how long they had been gone from the world they left behind.

"Reverie isn't what you think," Andrea said, ignoring the

Sandman's threat and loud enough that everyone turned toward her. "It isn't one long dream. I'm from the year 2020. My brother has been here for three years while our family couldn't find him. Many of you came here long before that. Do you remember? Do you remember how long it's been since you've come?"

A few of the children looked at the ground, while others murmured to one another. They shot Andrea suspicious glances, the black of their pupils reflecting the yellow of the Dream Clock and the real Sandman's smiling face.

"Who cares if this is all a beautiful unending dream," the Sandman bellowed. "Or how long you've been here. Children, what matters is that you remember *why* you came to Reverie in the first place."

The Sandman shot a sharp eye at Andrea. Andrea glared back. Her own eyes, she was sure, reflected the anger inside her, a bright fire, burning and billowing, untamed and ready to set something aflame.

"I am here," the Sandman continued, "because I lost my sister. My only beloved sister. She was irr-irreplaceable." His voice cracked. "I am here to remember her. I wanted to live in a world where I could have my sister by my side forever. In Reverie, I get to be all kinds of things. If I want, I can fly. I can hunt treasure. I can watch the first stars as they're born. Why would I ever want to go back to the place I left to come here? There was nothing there for me. I had no future. And you all are exactly the same. You all came here to remember, or to forget. *Remember*, children. I beg of you. *Remember* why you came."

The crowd of children stood, silent, soaking in the Sandman's words, remembering their own reasons. The cause that drew them to Reverie's gates. The thing that was enough for them to trade a dream for the chance at a night of escape. Andrea cast a glance at Francis, who stared at the crowd, his gaze flitting from person to person, like the eyes of the rabbit the neighbor's dog had once cornered in their garden.

Andrea found Penny, and Penny gave Andrea the smallest of nods. Enough to let her know they weren't alone.

"Just because life was hard for us back home . . ." Andrea paused and cleared her throat, hoping it might help her keep her shaking voice steady. Then she tried once more. "Life isn't supposed to be perfect. Sad things are going to happen, and we can't always slip out the back to escape them like in the Reverie tents. But we weren't meant to stay here. We were always meant to return home. If we stay in Reverie forever, we'll never know what would happen if we didn't run away from the hard parts. By avoiding the sadness, we lose the chance to live the good parts of life, too."

Andrea scanned the crowd. "I lost someone precious to

me to this place, and I can tell you for certain that there are people who wish more than anything that you would come home."

Many of the children glanced between Andrea and the ground, like they were fighting inside themselves about whether or not they wanted to believe her. If they wanted to stay tucked away in this delusion of a dream or if they wanted to believe they might still have a chance at real life, good times, bad times, and all. A few of the smaller children burst into tears.

"I choose to go home," Andrea said, unflinching. "Because I think there's something really, really beautiful in being able, through the good and the bad, to live life. *All* of it." She looked to Penny and smiled. "To have the chance to grow old."

"Do you?" the Sandman asked, creeping a few steps closer. The crowd parted as Andrea shuffled backward until she could feel the heat from a fiery nightmare lick the backs of her legs. "Do you *really* want to go home to a world where your brother is gone and your house is filled with the living ghosts of a family that used to exist?"

The Reverie children scowled and frowned. A flicker of hope burned inside Andrea's heart, that she might be able to win the rest of the children over. That they might want to go home, too.

"It's ungratefulness, that's what it is," the Sandman sneered. "You're all ungrateful, each and every one of you. Good thing I didn't create this world because I needed the children to be grateful. I created this world to give children a chance to escape their pain."

Andrea's blood ran hot at how heavily the Sandman was weighted down with lies. She shook her head. "You didn't *create* anything."

The crowd gasped.

"That's utter nonsense, you sniveling, pathetic child. How dare you seed such lies." The Sandman's placating *Ringmaster of Reverie* face faded, leaving an expression as cold as stone. As cold as his hands had felt when Andrea snatched away his umbrella.

As cold as a dream.

"*You're* the liar." Andrea and Francis took a step toward him. "You hid the ride that told the story of Reverie's beginnings—when the Dream Clock wasn't broken and the real Sandman was in charge and children went home at the end of each night. When you visited Reverie yourself and decided you shouldn't *ever* have to leave. You don't look anything like the Sandman on the Dream Clock, or the balloons, or the souvenirs. And I don't believe you're even showing your real face to us now."

A deep stillness and silence passed over the square. Not a child shuffled. Not a breeze stirred.

The Sandman exhaled and looked to the ground, placing a finger beneath his nose in an attempt to stifle a snicker. "You think you have *so many* answers. Think you've backed me into a corner. Umbrella-less, lie-less. You think you've made me out to be a fool." The Sandman swept his gaze down to the umbrella and took a step toward Andrea and Francis, further closing the gap between them.

Andrea pulled the umbrella tightly to her chest.

"I'll tell you what I *did* create," the Sandman continued. "Once, a very long time ago . . . or a very short time ago, depending on how you look at it, a young girl barged into *my* private dream, and with sorrow swimming in her eyes, she told me she had come here to forget. But when offered a chance to forget all her pain, in a very curious turn of events, she refused to take it.

"And I, knowing the hearts of all the children who enter Reverie's gates, knew your heart better than you knew yourself, Andrea. Even from that first encounter, I knew you hadn't come here to forget. I knew it was only a lie you told yourself. Because if you had, you would have taken me up on my offer." He tipped his head to the gray umbrella clutched in Andrea's hands. "I knew, deep, deep down, you wanted to *remember*."

"No," Andrea said. The Sandman might as well have stabbed her in the heart. The nagging, gnawing doubt that had crawled around inside her this whole time dug its ugly claws in until she fell to her knees.

The Sandman's brows arched, shrinking for a moment his otherwise striking forehead. "Well . . . in Reverie, here he is," the Sandman continued, twisting at the wound inside her. "I created the perfect wish for you. I even freed it from the confines of a tent. Your biggest dream, your perfect wish, is standing right beside you. He's right there. You can touch him and hug him and hear his voice. If you leave Reverie, all that," he waved his arms, "all this, including your precious brother . . . disappears forever."

Andrea pinched the inside of her cheek between her teeth until she tasted blood.

"Andrea," Francis whispered. Small beads of sweat formed on her brother's forehead. She wanted so badly to wipe them away, but she didn't want to lose her hold on the umbrella or give the Sandman a chance to swipe it back. Not after they had come so far.

Francis's anxious eyes turned to meet hers. "It's been hard sometimes, in this place, to know the difference between what's real and what's pretend. But if I'm not rea—" He swallowed. "If I'm a dream . . . then you never found me. I'm still out there. I'm still lost. If I'm real, we'll both be home soon. If I'm not . . . Please, don't give up everything to stay in a dream."

It was exactly the kind of thing the real Francis would say. And he was right.

She wouldn't do what the Sandman had done. In the real world, Margaret Grace was long gone, but the Sandman had chosen to stay here, surrounding himself with dream versions of his sister. Andrea wouldn't stay for a fake version of Francis, no matter how desperate she might once have been to escape the pain of losing him.

Andrea understood very much the despair that would have led the Sandman to do what he did. They were alike in many, many ways, as much as Andrea didn't want to admit it. But she also understood now just how sad it would be to choose to stay in that place forever. Where you never got to heal.

"Here you get to *keep* him. And I get to keep her." The Sandman turned to the smallest version of his sister, who stood staring at Andrea with clenched fists at the front of the crowd. "Why on earth would you choose to go back to a life filled with suffering?"

The rest of the Margaret Graces stepped forward from the crowd and formed a wall in front of the door to the Dream Clock. But unlike the resoluteness of their expressions the last time they met, this time the dream sisters' faces hinted at a sadness of their own. Maybe he had made them so much like the loving sister he had lost that some part of them wanted more for their brother. Maybe, even though they were a dream, the Margaret Graces hoped he might find healing, too.

"I don't want a fake brother," Andrea continued. "I want my real brother. I'll want him back every second of every day for the rest of my life." Andrea took a deep breath and exhaled it slowly. "But I don't want to live in a dream and hide from real life either. Not even from the hard parts, not anymore."

The Sandman, whose eyes just moments ago were lit up with hope, lowered as the expression on his face melted to sorrow.

Andrea held fast to the umbrella in one hand and reached out to Francis with the other. She no longer had any defenses to hide behind, but she would now place her trust in different things: in the relief that came after releasing a flood of tears; in the bittersweet memories of the good times, filled with kid sandwiches and love and their family, all together; in the healing work of time; and in the warmth of her brother's hand as he stood here beside her. The chance she had gotten, even if only in the world of a dream, to fight to bring home the one she had lost.

Andrea nodded to Penny, then opened the umbrella.

"What are you doing?" The Sandman lurched forward.

A wall of Reverie children jumped into action, forming a barrier between Andrea and the Sandman's desperate reach.

"This umbrella isn't yours any more than any other part of Reverie. It belongs to him." Andrea nodded at the picture of the man on the Dream Clock.

The umbrella opened to the dream sketch she had hoped to find inside, as if it, too, was eager to return to its true owner and desired to help Andrea find the way. She pulled out an aged, rough charcoal sketch of a lanky boy, maybe thirteen or fourteen, in dirty, patched-up clothes. And then next to him, a ringmaster in a fine tailored gray tuxedo and top hat with slicked-back salt-and-pepper hair.

He hadn't only built dream versions of Margaret Grace come back to life. He had also built himself a dream that covered up his own true identity, transforming a sad, grieving boy into a man who projected confidence, armed with magic and fit to run a circus built of dreams.

Andrea set the Sandman's dream aside, reaching into her pocket and pulling out the parchment, followed by the charcoal. She leaned against the dirt ground and drew in furious, heavy marks, transferring to paper everything she wanted for her wish and willing it into existence with the force of everything inside her.

The magic of Reverie began to stir as Andrea finished the

THE CIRCUS OF STOLEN DREAMS

drawing. It pulled toward her, then emanated back out from the umbrella in waves. The hopes of the children weaved in and tangled themselves up with its near-invisible threads. Hopes that something familiar would be waiting for them upon their return, and that all had not been lost, and that truth would win the day.

"I've figured out my perfect wish," Andrea said as she stood, opening the gray umbrella and sliding her parchment in among the others. "And it's waking up from this nightmare and finally going home."

AN UMBRELLA FULL OF DREAMS

Andrea stuck the point of the umbrella hard into the dirt, where it stood up on its own and began to spin. It unfolded as it spun, revealing dozens of thick, yellowed pieces of parchment attached to its underside, each paper bearing an image drawn in charcoal upon it. A sea monster with angry eyes and baring an open mouth full of teeth, the bubble dream she had walked past with the Sandman after they first met, with kids contained in tiny balls and floating with smiling faces. The umbrella continued to spin, faster and faster, and the dozens of pieces of paper turned into hundreds, then thousands, moving too fast now for anyone to catch a single image at a time.

The umbrella spun so fast it lifted from the dirt and flipped over right side up in the air above Andrea's head, then floated higher and higher until it must have been fifteen feet off the ground. Then Andrea saw it: dangling from a tightly tied piece of twine, straight down from the center of the umbrella, a black iron key swayed slowly in the middle of the wild flurry of parchment.

The entire crowd stared up at the spinning object in the sky, the only sounds around them the whir of the umbrella and the rustle of moving paper.

A gust of warm wind blew through Reverie's square, bringing with it ribbons of silver and blue that turned in the air like funnels. The wind kicked up clouds of dirt and Reverie debris: candy wrappers and bits of glitter and the scent of the first snow mixed with a summer rain. The top hat flew off the head of the fake Sandman, the drawing of his dream rose into the sky and disintegrated to dust, and the precise and confident ringmaster before them fell away to reveal the boy from the parchment. The crowd of Reverie children gasped once more. There he stood, a desperate boy, just like Andrea, who couldn't find his way and had forgotten himself in the depths of great loss. A boy who, unlike Andrea, had not yet found a way to heal.

The ribbons of silver and blue descended and wrapped themselves up around the fake Sandman and the dream versions of his sister. They grew wider, then joined together and billowed out like a balloon, lifting off the ground and looking more and more like a circus tent by the second.

Next the wild wind took the boy and his dreams inside the newly created tent, spinning them up and over the waving dream tent flags and the nightmares, which slowly retreated to the tents from which they came. The wind set them down in a vacant space just a short distance away, the place that the fake Sandman had offered to Andrea for her perfect wish.

Only then did the storm die down and the umbrella slow and float back into Andrea's waiting hand. She held it open long enough to tug the ebony key off its string, then snapped the umbrella shut.

"What did you do to him?" Francis asked, astonished.

"He's safe. And there's an exit to the dream, though it might not be easy for him to find it," Andrea said. "But besides that, it's not up to me to decide what happens to the boy who claimed to be the Sandman." She looked to the Dream Clock and to the friendly-looking face upon it. "It's up to the real one."

With the key in one hand and the umbrella in the other, Andrea walked to the tower. Penny pulled in alongside them. The Reverie children crowded in, too, waiting for whatever came next.

With shaking hands, Andrea held her breath and slid the key inside the lock, exhaling only when it turned and clicked.

The door creaked long and low as Andrea pulled it open, like a great metal yawn.

Before her stood a huge hill, a mini mountain of shimmering, glistening dream sand. Sand that thrummed with magic. Sand strong enough to put *anyone* into a deep and deathlike sleep.

Andrea had to hope that in this mountain, somewhere, rested the heartbeat of Reverie. That they would be able to find him, and wake him, and finally, finally go home.

"Penny, you know some of these kids, right?" Andrea looked back to her friend.

Penny nodded.

"They're going to have to be careful," Andrea said. "But we need some people who are willing to dig."

***

Several children, along with Penny, Andrea, and Francis, went to work on the sand, wearing goggles borrowed from a *Mad Scientist* dream. They dug their fingertips in deep and pushed it aside, still careful not to send any floating into the air.

A group of kids carried in heaps of burlap bags from one of the shops on the fairway. They bagged up the sand, tied the bags off, and passed them to others standing outside the tower, where more children waited to carry the sand and pile it up in the square. The work was long and hard and heavy, but a firm sense of hope buzzed in the air around them, and the children made progress quickly.

Andrea caught Penny sneaking off to one side and scooping a bit of sand into a small glass vial. Penny shrugged, only slightly embarrassed at being caught. "Just a trinket," she said before slipping the vial into her dress pocket. "Something to remember this place by."

Andrea was wiping the sweat off her forehead with her shirtsleeve when Francis yelled for her to come and see.

As Andrea grew closer, she saw what had made Francis call out: Still and silent, aged and ancient, and surrounded by silver dream dust lay the wrinkled, sleeping face of the man from the Dream Clock. The children in the tower gathered all around him and counted to three before lifting him, careful to turn away as the sand fell off his body and onto the floor. They hoisted him through the door and set him down on the ground in the square, while the frozen hand of the clock looked down on all of them, waiting.

Reverie's magic skittered around the square as if suddenly remembering what it once had been. But the Sandman's chest didn't move. Dream sand still sparkled in the full moon's light, all over his face. Someone handed Andrea a paintbrush. She went to work, tenderly brushing each grain from his ancient eyes.

"Please wake up," she whispered to the old man as she worked. "Please wake up. We need you to help us get home."

She teased the final grains out from a deep crease and fell back, setting the brush down on the earth. Andrea didn't know how long it would take for him to wake up—if waking up was even still possible for someone who had been buried in dream sand for so long.

All of Reverie stilled, frozen in expectation, until at last the old man took one great breath, a breath big enough to carry the universe inside it and also to cradle the smallest living creature and keep it safe.

And the world of Reverie—the dream tents, the children, and the clock tower—all exhaled with him in relief.

Andrea stood. Here he was. The real man behind Reverie. The one who could save them.

"My, look at all the children," he said, sitting up and taking note of the scattering of sand surrounding his body, the purple circles under the children's eyes, and the time on the Dream Clock.

He looked so fragile, so confused. So sad.

"Now, let's see . . ." A wrinkled hand moved upward, pulling off his nightcap and setting it down beside him. "The last thing I remember . . . a young man, a frequent visitor. A sad boy. It was time to go home. All the other children had left, but he refused. Then he snatched my umbrella. I've sustained quite the bump." The Sandman patted the spot where the umbrella must have met his head. "Then he dragged me to the tower. I must have fallen asleep as the Dream Clock chimed that it was time for the new children to come in." The Sandman's twinkling gaze landed on Andrea. "Tell me," he said. "How long have I been sleeping?"

So Andrea told him what she knew. She told him her story, and Francis's story, and as much of Reverie's story as she had uncovered during her time there. Penny helped fill in the gaps with her own tale and details Andrea hadn't yet had time to learn, while Francis and some of the other children chimed in as needed, too. They talked about the frozen clock, and the years that had gone by, and the missing children, and about how they all very much wanted to go home.

Finally, Andrea told him about how she had gotten hold of the umbrella and where his imposter could be found.

When they had finished, the Sandman shook his head and tsked, wiggling the toes inside his slippers, placing the cap back on his head, and raising a hand for Andrea to help him rise to his feet.

"I have quite the mess to clean up," he said, addressing all the children. "But it can be done, and it will be done, and it is none of your trouble."

Andrea handed the Sandman his magical umbrella. He gave a sad, small smile and took it from her, testing the weight of it in his arm.

"So heavy," he muttered, his words edged with regret. "Reverie is simply bursting with dreams." The Sandman turned back to the tower that had nearly become his tomb. "Oh, Hubert. How I wish things had gone differently for you."

Hubert. So that was the fake Sandman's name.

Snap.

Just then a great shift jarred the Dream Clock tower and the ground beside it. The children looked up to find the hand on the clock had moved, finally, one notch closer to *Awake*.

"We'll speed it up a bit tonight, children." The Sandman flicked a wrist at the clock, and it again lurched forward. "Some of you have been here nearly as long as I've been asleep, and I think we're long due for the light of morning."

Hope swelled in Andrea's chest, quickly followed by the icy fingertips of panic. Her eyes remained fixed on the clock while her hand reached blindly for Francis. He caught her arm and wrapped his own hands tightly around it.

"I'm pretty sure I'm real," Francis said, his words coming fast as another chime rang through the square. "I remember everything. I want to go home so bad. I've been here so long."

Her little brother laughed sadly to himself. "I can't tell any-more what's real and what's a dream, even if it's me."

"Well then," Andrea said. "I think it's past time we get you home."

Francis smiled, relieved. Andrea was glad for it. Even if he was about to fade away, Andrea wanted her last moments with her brother to be sweet and kind and laced with the love she would feel for him forever.

The sea of children followed the Sandman as he shuffled toward Reverie's gate. "So many new shops," he muttered. "Tsk, tsk, tsk."

Andrea ran her fingers along the wood of a nearby stall as they passed it by, a shop weighted and worn and rugged as textured pages. She suspected it was a Reverie original like the *Star Builder* dream and the rides that had been hidden away, which now could be restored into what they were always meant to be. As could Reverie itself.

The clock lurched forward again as the Sandman and the children reached Reverie's gate.

"It'll take some doing," the Sandman said, "but I wouldn't be me if I weren't able to play a little bit with time. I expect you'll all find yourselves in a home quite familiar." His wise eyes scanned the crowd. "You'll feel older, I'm afraid. Especially those of you who've been here quite long. The world will look the same, you will look the same, but you will find yourselves changed on the inside. I can't undo that . . ." His voice trailed off, tinged with sadness. "For some of you, your return will be more complicated than the rest."

He turned to Andrea, Penny, and Francis, and then passed his gaze over all those gathered at the gate. "Thank you, dear children, for all that you've done."

For so long Andrea had been frozen like the Dream Clock, trapped in the same place, unable to find escape, but that was all over now. She pressed her lips into a tight smile as a fresh set of tears fell down her cheeks. Tears that remembered her initial joy at finding this place. Her terror at realizing she could never go home. And all the healing her heart had done inside Reverie's walls, even though at times it had felt like she would never find her way through the pain.

The Sandman opened his umbrella and began distributing sheets of parchment to the children. "Your dreams," he said above the murmur of the crowd. "You bring them in when you arrive and take them with you when you go. You'll take them back in through the mouth. Let them dissolve on your tongue."

"We *eat* our dreams?" Francis asked as the Sandman handed him his nightmare sketch.

The Sandman chuckled and gave an exaggerated wink. "They don't taste like paper, I promise."

Penny received her dream and took a bite. She inhaled as a signature Penny Periwinkle look of pure delight spread across her face.

"It tastes like brown sugar and toasted marshmallow and . . ." She rolled it around on her tongue. "Root beer float!" Her smile faded when she saw Francis holding his dream with tentative, shaky hands.

"Go on." Andrea nudged her brother with a gentle elbow. "He said it wouldn't taste bad."

Francis grimaced, then balled the dream together and stuffed it in his mouth, swallowing it down fast.

"Well?" Penny, having just finished her own dream, stuck a hand on her hip and waited for Francis's response.

"It tasted . . . like black licorice." Francis curled a lip but seemed to be doing all right, given the fact that he had eaten a nightmare.

Now it was Andrea's turn. Her dream, the memory of the night they lost Francis, melted on her tongue, flavored with milky moonlight and vanilla and crisping leaves in the fall.

"It's almost time," Penny said to her friends, a wistful look on her face as the clock once again chimed.

"Will you be okay?" Andrea's heart pinched. "Will you be lonely when you return?"

Penny sighed. "It won't be easy for me when I go back.

I guess I could come here again, if I wanted, but I think it's worth it to wait for the real friends who care for you just as you are, even if they don't show up right away." She took Andrea's and Francis's hands and squeezed them one final time before letting go. "Because I know that people *are* out there, somewhere in the tangled mess of space and time, waiting to be my friend."

Andrea gave Penny a hug and wiped a tear from the corner of her eye.

Having handed back all the dreams, the Sandman made his way back to Reverie's gates. He cleared his throat, and the murmuring crowd hushed at the sound. The bells on the clock chimed, and the Sandman began to sing, soft and soothing, a lullaby Andrea had heard once before.

"Return, dear ones, to where you came.
May this sweet reprieve give you strength."

The gate to Reverie creaked slowly open. The children crowded closer, their bodies warm and worn. Their hearts ready to return home.

"Should your heart tomorrow be once more built of sorrow,
Take comfort and here return once again."

"It won't be perfect," Andrea said quickly to her brother once the Sandman finished singing. Now *she* was the one talking like the hourglass was nearly empty. "Our family will look different than we wanted. But there's no way I'm going home without my little shadow. We'll always have each other."

Please, Andrea thought. There was no chance she'd ever make the mistake again of thinking that running away from her problems would somehow fix them. She had to hold on to the hope that there would be good memories to build once she returned. Memories that would help heal the holes that were there for now and help her to live with the bittersweet holes that would ever remain.

Though she had once thought herself too old for wishing on stars, Andrea turned toward to the sky and found one of the small, blinking pricks of light in the darkness. She closed her eyes and wished on that star. Right then. Right there. Wished that the warmth she felt when she held Francis's hand meant he was real and not one of Hubert's wish creations. That when she finally did wake up from Reverie, Francis would be there by her side. But she wouldn't know for sure until it was finished. And the only way home was to continue walking forward, even through the pain.

Please. Andrea begged, from the wild beating of her tender heart. *Please let him be real. Let us both go home.*

With Francis's hand still warm in hers, Andrea looked back at Reverie one final time. The other Reverie children watched from where they stood, their eyes no longer dew-filled and dreamy but awake and crystal clear. The wise old Sandman smiled at them in his silly pajamas and slippers and cap.

And a scent like the salted air before a rainstorm blew through the fairway, a strong wind swirling around them as a tornado of raindrops and sleep sand and tears and dreams and nightmares fell from the sky.

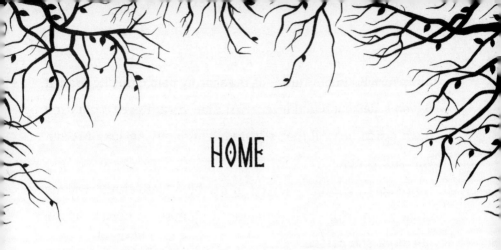

HOME

Andrea peeled her eyes open. The morning light shone through her window, much brighter than usual, like she had spent a long, long time in the dark and someone now shined a flashlight right in her face.

One by one, pieces pulled themselves together to form a picture. Francis. Her parents. Reverie. The faux ringmaster and Dream Clocks and locked iron gates. A world filled with contradictions: nightmares that bled from circus tents and dreams where kids could fly.

"Francis!" Andrea slid off the top bunk and peered down at her brother's bed.

Empty.

Her heart dropped to the floor. It would have felt better if someone had crushed it with a rock. The window stood open, without any hint of frost. But Francis wasn't there. A lump formed in her throat as the searing pain of losing Francis flayed her like it had the very first time, creating a fresh wound deep inside her. All that. All the nightmares. And her brother was still gone.

Andrea wrapped herself in her blue blanket and walked quietly down the hall, catching a glimpse of herself in the mirror as she passed.

There she came to a stop.

Wide-eyed and openmouthed, Andrea placed a hand to her face. The girl who peered back at her from the mirror wasn't twelve. She was tall for her age, her hair shorter than she would like, but this girl was only nine. The age she had been when Francis disappeared.

A surge of hope blew through Andrea's soul. She bolted down the stairs, every muscle tight as she bounded multiple steps at a time and burst into the kitchen.

The digital calendar read October 22, 2017. The day after Francis disappeared.

But there sat her little brother, eating breakfast at the table.

"Ah, there you are," her mother said. "Francis was telling me how you helped him through a bad dream last night," Andrea's mom ruffled Francis's hair.

"Mom!" Francis said, with just a hint of a smile.

The doorbell sounded and Andrea's mom went to the door and opened it, letting Andrea's father inside.

"Good morning, sunshines," he said, his voice a tad too cheerful. He set his jaw and looked over at his children, a cloud of sadness brushing over his eyes. "I'm here to pick up a few more of my things," he said. "Then your mom and I thought it might be nice if I took you kids to the park."

"Okay," Francis said, shifting in his seat and staring hard at his bowl as he shoved another spoonful of cereal into his mouth.

Andrea couldn't even speak. Every single thing she had experienced had felt *so long*. Years' worth of time. And yet, here they were at the start again, but also at the ending. A completely different ending to their story.

Andrea bolted to her brother and hugged him until she was sure she had squished out all the air. As if he had been waiting for this moment, Francis dropped his spoon in the bowl of now mostly milk and hugged her tightly in return.

There in Andrea's arms was proof that everything she'd been through had been worth it. She had done something very, very hard and hadn't broken. And most important of all, she had really, truly found her brother and brought him home.

Mid-hug, Andrea's mother pulled in behind them and wrapped her arms around Andrea and Francis. Her father rushed forward, bending down and joining the hug on the other side, their bodies wrapping the children in a cocoon of warmth.

Andrea's eyes filled with tears.

"We love you both, and we'll get through this together," her dad said, resting his cheek on Francis's hair. "You two are our whole world."

"We . . ." Francis began, his voice at almost a whisper.

"Are . . ." Andrea joined him, pressing her forehead into his.

"A family." The foursome finished together, the final word hanging in the air, lingering in the otherwise silent kitchen.

"We're still your family, my loves." Andrea's mother kissed the top of her head. "We will *always* be your family."

There would be no midnight dances in the kitchen, as there had been in the Sandman's dream. But there could be this.

Andrea took in an unsteady breath and let the lingering sadness float away as she exhaled. Things would never be the same as they were when their family was together, but that didn't mean she was loved any less. If she let that be her anchor, when the sadness arrived again in waves, she would be better able to keep it in balance. And there would be happy times, too, still to come. More memories to be made with her mom and her dad and her brother. Even if they looked different from before.

Her father gave an extra squeeze and looked away, blinking his own eyes fast, then wiping a single tear as he walked up the stairs to gather his things, and her mother returned to her cup of coffee.

Andrea hesitated a moment more, then pulled back from Francis and slipped her hand inside the pocket of her pajamas. Her fingers brushed against two items inside, something soft and something smooth. Her heart sped up as she pulled out a ruby-red feather and a single gold coin. The memories of *Soar* came rushing back. The fierce wind, the feeling of slicing a cloud, her laugh as she and Penny took flight.

Andrea jumped as the sound of the doorbell echoed again through the house.

"Geesh, Drea, it's just the door," Francis teased.

"I'll get it." Their mom went to the door and opened it.

After a few moments, Andrea's mom called out. "Andrea, sweetie, can you come here, please?"

Andrea's breath caught in her chest when she saw who stood in the entryway to their house.

Ms. Penelope. Their nosy neighbor. With hints of strawberry in her graying hair, and a full figure, and eager eyes.

Looking a bit different as an adult but recognizable just the same, Penny Periwinkle had, indeed, become an old woman. She wore small reading glasses perched on the tip of her nose and maintained her rosy, rosy cheeks, now framed by wrinkles. *Smile lines.* Penny had returned to her own life as a child. And she had had a happy life.

"Oh, Andrea, I'm so glad you're awake!" she said. "I left something for you yesterday . . . It was just a trinket, but I wanted to make sure you found it all right."

Andrea furrowed her brow, wondering what on earth Penny would have left for her—

Just a trinket.

Andrea considered the words and gasped. Her memory flashed back to the vial of sand Penny had collected in the Dream Clock tower and stuffed into her pocket. Just like the vial of sand Andrea had found on the windowsill the night Francis disappeared.

She didn't know how many times the world could flip upside down on a girl in one morning, but here was the last piece of Reverie's puzzle, standing in the entryway to her house, and she wasn't a nosy neighbor at all. She was Andrea's friend, who had been looking out for her this whole entire time. A friend who had waited patiently all those years, keeping the sand safe and knowing Andrea would need it to find her way through Reverie and to help them all get home.

"Yes," Andrea said, her mind reeling. "I found it. Thank you."

"Well, I hope you found it useful." Penny—*Ms. Penelope* gave Andrea a secret wink and handed her a tin of shortbread cookies.

Wide-eyed and at a complete loss for words, Andrea nodded and accepted the gift.

"My own grandchildren are coming to visit, and it seems I've made too many. Silly me." She smiled down at Francis, who smiled back like she was a familiar face to him, too. Someone more friend than neighbor.

"Maybe you could meet my grandchildren one day," Ms. Penelope continued. "They're about your age, you know, and I think you'd get along nicely. I could set out lemonade and cookies and give you some time to get to know each other. I'm quite certain they are always happy to make new friends."

Andrea and Francis shared a secret look, and Francis said that sounded nice.

Andrea's heart ballooned with gratitude. It rested inside her like a warm cup of hot chocolate on a cold winter's day. She clutched the tin of cookies and winked back at Ms. Penelope, her good, old friend.

Once the door had closed and Ms. Penelope had made her way back across the street, Andrea returned to the kitchen. She looked forward to visiting her friend soon, when they could talk openly and freely about what happened to them.

About what life had been like for her once she got home. And all they had been through together.

***

Andrea and Francis had time to talk in the lull after breakfast and before their father was ready to take them to the park. They hid away in their bedroom as their dad moved more boxes of his stuff into the back of his SUV. They wouldn't have wanted to watch that happen anyway, even if they didn't have to do something more important.

The two of them talked about everything as they sat on the floor and leaned against the bottom bunk. They had survived a nightmare, and the reality that existed for them now would still hurt a lot, in many ways. Andrea rested in the fact that she had chosen this and that whatever the future might hold, at least she and Francis would face it together.

Even though she couldn't erase everything they had lost, and even though she had known the risk that she might have woken up without Francis, living this, her real life, was better than believing the lie that it was better to run away.

"What did you make as the door?" Francis asked. He stood and began rearranging the pictures on his dresser. "For the dream you trapped the fake Sandman in. How did you know he wouldn't get out right away and keep us all trapped?"

"I made the door so that if he found it, he wouldn't be a danger anymore," she said, thinking back to the sad look on the dream sisters' faces in the moments before she created the dream. "In order for him to get out of the tent, he would have had to learn to say goodbye."

Francis paused and stared straight ahead a moment before nodding and continuing to play with the arrangement of the pictures. "And what do you think the real Sandman did to the fake one?"

Andrea hadn't yet given a thought about what would happen once she handed the real Sandman his umbrella. Maybe Hubert was still in Reverie, working things out inside the tent, learning to say goodbye to his sister. Or maybe the Sandman had handled things a different way. Andrea hoped the boy who had pretended to be the Sandman had been able to find healing, one way or another.

Andrea shrugged. "Wherever he is, the real Sandman is back in charge. Everything is back the way it should be." Andrea tried to convince herself as much as Francis. The room took on a slight chill as Andrea considered the possibility that Hubert might still be out there, somewhere, about to cause some trouble.

"Oh," Francis said, seemingly satisfied. "Right." He stood

and straightened out his clothes. "I'm going outside to play while we wait."

Andrea stared at the bottom bunk. The empty bed she had stared at for three years that once again would hold her brother each night. A bed that had never really been empty at all now that they were living in a world where Francis had never disappeared.

"Okay." Andrea bit the inside of her lip as Francis bounced out of the room, uncomfortable at the thought of letting him out of her sight after everything that had happened. She ran down the hall and to the open window that looked over their backyard. She breathed in the crisp fall air and watched her brother as he climbed on a swing and pumped his legs, building momentum. She tested the breeze, searched it for any hint of the aroma that had carried them both to Reverie in the first place. But the wind only carried with it the scent of decaying leaves and a neighbor's fresh cut grass.

Then she smiled as she pinched herself. Good and hard, just to be safe.

ACKNOWLEDGMENTS

To my husband, John Paul Savaryn. Thank you for encouraging me to finish my novel, and for reading through multiple drafts of the two manuscripts it took to get to this point. Thank you for loving me so well. You play such a huge role in making our marriage one where I have the space to be my best self and to dream big. Your unwavering belief that I would succeed in being a published author has meant the world, especially during the moments when I doubted myself or felt discouraged. Thanks for supporting this dream in word and deed, for watching the kids so I could carve out time to write, and for your support in hiring child care so I could pursue my dream long before I sold this book. You are my favorite person and the best partner I could have ever hoped to walk through this life with. The life we have built and the family we have made together is my absolute perfect wish.

To my children, I am so grateful for your wild imaginations and for your relationships with each other, both of which I'm sure will be an endless source of inspiration for me as a writer for years to come. Felicity, thanks for sharing with me a few seeds that grew into some of the magical elements of this story, including the dizzying suckers and *The Frigid Place*.

To my parents, Gary Wondrash and Linda Steber, and to my stepparents, Carrie Wondrash and Tom Steber. Dad, you taught me the value of hard work and of sticking with something even if it isn't easy, which served me so well as I wrote this book. Mom, you have been my constant cheerleader in life, and it's been so much fun to share in the excitement of this journey with you. Carrie and Tom, I'm so thankful for you both, and your support of this dream has encouraged me greatly.

To my spectacular mentors, Juliana Brandt and Lacee Little. I am still so amazed that you chose me and my dream circus story to mentor in Pitch Wars 2018. I felt your love and support from the moment mentees were announced, through each word of your editorial letters and feedback, and in all our conversations during Pitch Wars and since. I admire you both and am incredibly blessed to know you. Your mentorship and friendship have changed my life and made it possible for this dream to come true.

To my amazing agent, Chloe Seager. Thank you for championing me as an author and for finding this story its perfect editor and publishing house home. I knew from our first phone conversation that we would have a great partnership, and I look forward to what's to come.

To my editor, Liza Kaplan. The moment Chloe told me

about your enthusiasm for my story, I hoped so hard that it would work out for *The Circus of Stolen Dreams* to be published by Philomel. Your wise insights have helped bring out the best in my work, and I couldn't have hoped for a better partner in this process. Thank you also to Talia Benamy, and the entire team at Penguin Random House who has had a hand in bringing this book to life. Samira Iravani and Matt Saunders, thank you for the gorgeous cover design and art, which are such a perfect match for this book. Thank you as well to Monique Sterling, Janet Pascal, Kate Frentzel, Marinda Valenti, and Tricia Callahan.

To Brenda Drake. I hope to meet you in person one day, but please know that I am so grateful that you created Pitch Wars. It has been such an honor to have had the chance to be a mentee. It's why this book is here in published form today.

To the Pitch Wars class of 2018, especially Tiffany Liu, Megan Clements, Ellen Stonaker, Mindy Thompson, Summer Rachel Short, and Jessica S. Olson. Thank you for your encouragement during Pitch Wars and beyond. It has been such a gift to be a part of our supportive community, and I so look forward to celebrating the many successes that are to come in the future for us.

To the many writers who have supported me along the

way. Catherine Bakewell, you are my friend and an amazing CP. It is a joy to walk this journey with you. Thank you for reading *The Circus of Stolen Dreams* and telling me it was special. To Sam B. Farkas, thank you for your insights on an early version of this story, and for your enthusiasm about its potential. Thank you, also, for advising me to be patient and to trust that there were better things to come, and for suggesting the Sandman set the nightmares free. Susan Bishop Crispell, thank you for being one of the first authors I ever connected with in the writing community. Thanks for taking the time to offer me constructive feedback and encouragement when I still had a long way to go. Allison Mullinax, thank you for your kindness and support along the way. Sabina Fidahić, thank you for reading my first draft of this story and offering such positive feedback. Alyssa Colman, Cyla Panin, and Rachel Greenlaw, I'm so glad to know you. Thanks for the solidarity and also for the chats about navigating the publishing waters and other life things. I look forward to many more in the future.

To Kurt Hartwig and Bronwyn Clark. Your CP feedback during Pitch Wars was filled with wisdom. It helped strengthen my manuscript in so many ways. Thank you for taking the time to read my words and for being a part of this story.

To Professor Valerie Laken at UW–Milwaukee. Thank you for offering me honest and helpful feedback when I turned in some very rough short stories in my first class with you. You could have easily written me off as a lost cause, but because you didn't, I was able to see myself improve, and I was able to harbor hope that I could pursue becoming an author someday. Thank you for your thoughtful courses that built a strong foundation for me to grow my craft, and for pushing me to become better in such constructive ways.

To Kyle Wondrash. Thank you for being so excited for your big sister and for being the reason I know what it feels like to have a little brother. To Marta Knodle and the entire Savaryn family. Thanks for listening to me talk about writing a lot, and for celebrating all the good news.

To Hanna Tschida, Keliana Licup, Rebecca Nelson, Terri Lynch, Monica Braun, Linda Steber, Carrie Wondrash, and Catherine Wahl. Thanks for reading my very first manuscript and encouraging me to continue on the writerly path.

To my aunt, Jeannine Liebert. Like Andrea finds her way to healing in the story, writing *The Circus of Stolen Dreams* became part of my own healing journey in the months after we lost you. Miss you all the time.

To Butterfly Books in De Pere, Wisconsin. Working there was the perfect job for a bookworm teenager like myself. How

I wish it were still around for me to visit today, and it will forever hold a special place in my heart. I would have loved to have seen my book on one of the bookshelves I used to dust or in one of the window displays I used to create.

To the teachers and librarians along the way who fostered my love of reading and who taught me that the magic of stories is real.

To Starbucks, for much of the coffee that fueled the creation of this novel.

And to God, from whom all creativity flows.